FOR THE LOVE OF GOGO

A Novella

Tracy Gray

ISBN-13: 9798672833552

Cover design by: Kerry Sovde Design
Cover Model: Caprice Cole
Front Cover Art Photographer: Maria Peterson
Back Cover Art Photographer: Tracy Gray-Caruthers
Editing by: LRB1 Style! Editing Services
Library of Congress Control Number: 2018675309
Printed in the United States of America

This book is dedicated to every person who wouldn't let me walk away from writing - specifically Shwanda Cross; Latricia Samson; Renee Moore; Chermell Ellis; Martine "Pudding" Powell; Ciera Caruthers; Tanyanika Conaway and LaDwyna Hoover.

Also to those who supported the (don't call it a) come back - Jackie Nichols; LaShann Rochelle-Bailey; Loretta Harris-Wright; Brandy Means and Angela David.

Thank you!

CONTENTS

FOREWORD

When I sat down to write this story, after sooooooo many years of not writing at all, my only goal was to tell a story that was the epitome of light & love.

This is a light read that I hope evokes smiles and feelings of happiness. A perfect summertime read.

I hope you enjoy reading this story as much as I enjoyed crafting it.

With lightheartedness,

~ Tracy Gray

"For the Love of GoGo is a novella, which means that by it's very nature, it is shorter than a full-length novel.

Having said that, please note that it does have a beginning, a middle, and an ending. However, the story wraps up in just over 100 pages.

If full-length novels are more to your liking, please feel free to check out other Tracy Gray offerings.

CHAPTER 1

Indigo

It started with stereotypical behavior.

Like most people of color, I disliked stereotypes. And I particularly disliked feeding into one, instead I prided myself on railing against stereotypes and proving them wrong. But in this one particular area, I just couldn't seem to help myself, because I liked what I liked.

So what if my own skin complexion was often referred to as "high-yellow", "red-bone", or "light-bright-and-damn-near-white?" Did the fact that I tended to prefer dark-skinned men to light-skinned ones really make me a stereotype?

Okay. Okay. I didn't just ***tend*** to prefer them. I ***always*** preferred them. And it wasn't just that I had a preference for dark-skinned men, it was the phenomenon that always seemed to occur. It was the strange, but unavoidable phenomenon that whenever a dark-skinned man was within a hundred mile radius, their mere presence always drew my attention.

It was a weird and unwelcomed magnetism that I didn't want or ask for, but always found myself caught up in. Even when the guy was unattractive, I still found myself at least momentarily enraptured by the chocolatey goodness of his skin.

I didn't know what that was. I didn't know how to fight it. All I knew was that whenever I encountered that dark, dark skin, I couldn't help staring. It was so rude, but I couldn't help admiring the creamy smoothness that only seemed achievable by those who possessed the most highly of "melanated" shades.

It was my absolute weakness.

So, that was what I was doing at the moment. Staring at the "blue-black" brother across the hotel lobby. I couldn't make out his features, per se. Couldn't tell if he was actually good-looking, or simply my preference, but he was definitely assembled in the way that I liked my men packaged. He was tall, with a medium, yet muscular build...and he was very, very dark-skinned.

"Que devrions-nous manger pour le diner?" My twin sister, Clarke questioned, diverting my attention away from the black beauty.

"Uhm." I considered where I wanted to have dinner. "Maybe at..." I began.

"En francais." Clarke admonished. "Say it in French, GoGo."

I nodded my head. Clarke and I were in Paris. It was my idea that we take the trip to France for Paris Fashion Week. During the four days that we were there, - my twin and I had an absolute blast attending fashion shows during the day and partying at night.

I'm a successful social media personality, and beauty influencer. My YouTube, Twitter and Instagram channels, @GoGoGoesGlam, all have well over two million followers each, giving me both fans and foes all over the world.

Clarke and I actually came to Paris on the dime of one of my sponsors. Because of that, I'd done my due diligence like the professional that I am, and recorded, filmed, vlogged, and live-streamed my experiences in Paris for three straight days. I immersed myself in fashion, beauty, nightlife and even a bit of debauchery, all for the pleasure of those who subscribed, followed, or randomly visited any of my online spaces.

By the time I was done memorializing my time in the city of light, I had enough content to do a week-long series on my Paris trip. I would never do that to my subscribers (how boring would that be), but the point was that I had enough material to do it.

Just like it was my idea that Clarke and I make the trip to Paris, I was also the one who suggested that we use the trip as an opportunity to practice our French.

Clarke was much better at speaking the language than I was. Then again, I spent most of my time in French class (and school in general) chatting with friends, flirting with boys and basically being a social butterfly. As I got older, and developed a desire to become a more well-rounded and cultured individual, things started to get real. I regretted not taking advantage of the opportunity to learn the language more seriously when I was in school. And since even the Rosetta Stone package I purchased wasn't helpful enough, I ended up having to use some of my "YouTube money" (as my daddy referred to it) to hire a private French tutor to prepare for the trip.

So, here we were, in Paris, France on our final night trying to figure out where to have dinner.

"Et Chez Andre?" I suggested a restaurant that one of my influencer friends had recommended.

"Qu'en est-il d'Ellsworth?" Clarke asked.

I couldn't say that I was surprised that my sister suggested Ellsworth. It had obviously become her favorite restaurant in Paris, but I still gave her the screw face. Hell, we had already eaten there twice in the last four days. I told her so, in French.

"Nous y avons deja mange deux fois." I held up 2 fingers for emphasis.

"Mais c'est delicieux." Clarke protested with a whine.

It was irrelevant to me that it was delicious. I wasn't eating there again. It was our last night in Paris. I wanted to experience something new. Something different.

"Excuse me." Came the deep timbre of the voice.

And I just knew. I knew exactly who that voice belonged to, before I even turned my head, because Jon B.'s "Cocoa Brown" started to play in my mind. It was of course, the phenomenon of the deep-dark chocolate. That was how Clarke and I referred to it amongst ourselves, "the phenomenon of the deep-dark chocolate."

"Bonjour." I chirped (over the sound of Jon B's. smooth tenor in my head) in an inflection so perfectly spot on Parisian, that I almost physically patted myself on the back.

The man standing in front of me was truly perfection. He was everything that I liked, wrapped up just the way I liked it.

Of course he was chocolatey. That went without saying. And yes, he was tall. He was at least 6'3 or so, but he was also handsome. The guy was clearly all man, but he had a boyish face. A baby face. Kind of chubby cheeks, full lips, a full beard and bright, happy, milk chocolate colored eyes. He wasn't smiling at the moment, but I could just tell that smiles from this man were gorgeous, and easy.

I leaned over to Clarke and said, "maintenant, il est delicieux." I knew dude heard me, but I guess I hoped that he didn't speak French. Or maybe I hoped that he did, and would understand what I had just told my sister. Which loosely translated to, "now, *he is* delicious."

"Hi." Clarke said to the gentleman.

His face slid into a beautiful smile, just like I knew it would. And right away, I noticed his dimples. I always noticed dimples, because I was a sucker for them. Particularly dimples as deep as this guy's.

"You speak English." He sounded relieved.

"I speak English." Clarke confirmed with a nod and a smirk.

I stayed silent.

"You're American." It was a statement, not a question.

She nodded again. There was no doubt that her Midwestern accent had given that little nugget of information away immediately. There was no mistaking Clarke for a European once she opened her mouth. "As are you."

He nodded. "I don't mean to bother you, or interrupt..."

Clarke waved him off in that casual way that she had about her. "You're good. What's up?"

He hesitated, but then decided to press ahead. "Uhm, I'm just wondering if you'll tell your friend that she's beautiful. No disrespect, and I don't usually do this kind of thing..."

"Uhm huhm, sure you don't." Clarke semi-teased. "You mean

you don't usually fight your way across crowded hotel lobbies to feed bullshit to complete strangers?"

He chuckled and ran his hand over his beard. "Nah. I don't. And I promise that I'm not trying to feed her...or you bullshit. She's just..." he looked over at me. "She's gorgeous. She caught my attention, and I had to come over here. It was like...magnetic."

Clarke looked from the stranger to me with a smirk that was threatening to turn into a full-blown grin playing at her lips. Finally, she shook her head back and forth slowly. "Ugh. Men and game."

"It's not game." He assured her.

She heaved out a sigh. "You're lucky you seem sincere. And that my "friend" is taking me to dinner at my favorite restaurant tonight."

I almost broke character right then and there to assure her that we would not be eating at Ellsworth this evening, and I damn sure wouldn't be paying for her meal regardless of where we chose to eat.

Clarke huffed out another sigh of exasperation, mostly because she was dramatic, but also because she was easily annoyed. "I will translate your bullshit, sir."

At this, the stranger laughed out loud. I liked the sound. Deep, hearty and rich. This was a man who was confident in and comfortable with himself. If there was one thing that I appreciated, it was a person who did not take themselves too seriously.

"Thanks." The grin remained on his handsome face.

"What's your name, Super Star?"

He gave Clarke another easy chuckle. "Oh, I'm just a fuckboy to you, now? Should I just walk away?"

My sister knew me. So, she knew that I was standing there waiting with bated breath to be introduced to the man who thought I was so beautiful, that he had sought me out to tell me so. There was no way she would run him off, or let him leave before I got my ego stroked.

"No. No." She told him. "I'm just messing with you. I'm gonna translate your message to her. I just need to know your name."

"Northern. My name is Northern."

"Okay, Northern. Here goes."

I fought my hardest not to laugh or smile at Clarke when she turned to look at me. I knew good and damn well that she was not going to translate that Northern thought I was beautiful. It was the anticipation of what outrageousness might come from between her lips that had my insides already racking with suppressed laughter.

"Uhm," she began, in a very American, typically black girl way. "Je parie que tu cremes ta culotte, maintenant."

I couldn't stop myself. I dissolved into giggles at her telling me, "Uhm, I bet you're creaming your panties, right now."

I really hoped that Northern wouldn't take offense to my laughter. But it certainly didn't help matters that Clarke, too, had dissolved into her own fit of giggles.

I dropped the façade of being Parisian and spoke to my sister in English. "You know I can't stand you, right?"

"It's true, though." She insisted, still laughing. "I know you, so I know it's true."

I looked up at Northern just as his handsome features turned dark with a frown.

I reached my hand out towards him, although I didn't actually touch him. "I'm sorry. Please don't walk away. We're silly with each other. We should not have included you in our bad behavior. It wasn't fair, and it was rude."

"Yeah." Clarke agreed, regaining her composure. "It *was* rude, and our mother raised us better than this."

He watched us in silence. In all honesty, he probably wasn't sure how to react to the fact that we were having a good laugh at his expense. I watched him decide how to handle the situation.

"I'm tripping, because I can't really tell if you're shitting on me, or if I'm just caught in the middle of you two entertaining each other." He said finally.

"The second one." Clarke assured him. "Definitely the second one. We're not trying to shit on you."

I hated the thought that I was responsible for causing those glorious features to morph into something that wasn't so attractive.

"Sorry. For real, I'm sorry." I said softly. "And thank you for thinking that I'm beautiful."

If he chose to walk away, I at least wanted him to know that I appreciated his determination to get that information to me.

Northern shook his head. "It's not an opinion. You're beautiful. You're a beautiful woman."

I did a slow, appreciative perusal of the male specimen that was Northern. I started at his feet, and let my eyes roam up slowly, until my gaze made it to his handsome face. I rested my gaze there for a few seconds, as if committing his features to memory. "And you are a beautiful man."

Northern gave me a warm smile. "So, you speak English?"

I couldn't help blushing as I felt the warm heat of embarrassment wash over me. "I do. I'm from America." The blush deepened. I couldn't believe how badly I was coming off in front of somebody so gorgeous. *I'm from America? What kind of dumb shit was that to say?*

Clarke, who was never one to let me get away with anything, prepared for the roasting. "You're from America? Oh damn, GoGo. Come on. Stop being so awkward."

I took a deep breath and turned to Northern. "I'm sorry. I'm embarrassed, because I was being shady, pretending not to speak English and you caught me. When you walked over, I really just wanted to see where the conversation was gonna go, and before I knew it, I had committed to the role of 'Parisian girl'." I held up my fingers and made air-quotes.

Northern chuckled softly, deep in his throat. "Okay. Okay." He acquiesced. "So, Parisian girl, what's your name?"

"Indigo." I gestured towards my sister. "And this is my twin, Clarke."

He stared at us silently for a moment. "Indigo and Clarke?"

"Actually, it's Clarke and Indigo." She corrected. "I was first."

"Yes." I agreed on a sigh. "By four *whole* minutes. I know. I was there."

Northern didn't comment on our bickering. "Clarke and Indigo from..."

"*Mo' Better Blues*." I supplied.

"Our mother is on some "Denzel for life" type stuff. So she named us after the two women that he couldn't choose between in that movie." Clarke added.

"But didn't he actually end up choosing?" Northern questioned.

"Clarke doesn't like to talk about that, since he chose...Indigo!" I announced loudly.

"Only because she had that kid."

"Doesn't matter. He still chose her."

"Whatever, we don't talk about that." Clarke replied. Then she looked up at Northern. "It's been really great meeting you and chatting with you Super Star, but I'm starving, and we were about to head out to find dinner."

"Is that an invitation?" He asked.

Her eyes widened. "Okay. So, you tried to convince me that you don't usually talk to strange women, but you don't seem to have a problem with inviting yourself out to dinner with strange women."

"I never said that I don't talk to strangers. What I said was that I don't usually make my way across crowded hotel lobbies to tell them that they're beautiful."

"Whatever, Northern. You're welcome to come with us." She told him. "As long as you're paying. You're American. Hell, you know nothing in life is free."

Northern looked around the lobby for a moment before speaking. "It's just the two of you, right? Like a whole squad is not about to come outta the woodwork?"

Clarke considered him for a few seconds. "So, speaking of 'squads', where's your squad, Northern? You didn't just roll up in Paris alone, did you?"

"Nah. Not at all. I came here for work. Fashion week was

work for me. Fashion week is always work for me. So, I definitely came with a squad. And I've been with them for 5 straight days. I need a break. I need to talk about something other than...work. Other than expectations and responsibilities."

I completely understood what he meant, and fleetingly wondered if he was an influencer, too.

"Well, we're headed for Ellsworth." Clarke said.

"We're headed for Chez Andre." I corrected. And when she gave me the eye, I added, "I mean, hell, the only reason Northern even came over to us is because I'm beautiful. So, I should get to choose the restaurant."

"I'm the one who got him to agree to pay for dinner. I'm choosing." My sister insisted.

"Damn. Do I exist, or nah?" He asked with a chuckle.

I looked up at him. "You wanna be the tie-breaker?"

"I don't know. Do I? I don't know if I wanna get between twins."

"We're fraternal twins. We're not that close." Clarke joked.

"Bullshit." Northern responded. Then he looked down at me, again and I met his gaze. I might've smoldered at him, licked my lips and batted my brown eyes a little bit. "Chez Andre." He concluded.

"Yes." I said victoriously.

Northern laughed and shook his head.

"Well, hell." Clarke threw her hands up in the air. "I saw that coming a mile away."

The three of us slipped inside of a cab. Somehow, I ended up in the middle, with Clarke on my left side, and Northern on my right. His leg rested against mine and the warmth from his body set off butterflies in my stomach.

I wasn't generally the type to hang out with strangers at home in America, and definitely not in foreign countries. I considered that risky behavior, and I wasn't trying to find myself in a missing person situation. I mean, I felt "safer" because Clarke was with me. We had both taken self-defense classes and knew how to hurt somebody, but I normally wouldn't even put myself in a position where I thought I was going to need to use self-defense techniques. And I didn't think I would need them with Northern. He had good energy...positive energy that completely drew me in.

His hands were resting in his own lap when I picked up the one closest to me and held it, lacing my fingers between his. I couldn't have verbally expressed why, but I wanted to touch him. He looked over at me and our eyes met. I wasn't sure if it was my imagination, but I felt like we were vibing like crazy. When he leaned over and kissed me lightly on the cheek, I knew I wasn't imagining it. I wanted to repay his kiss on the cheek with one on the lips, but I commanded myself to behave. Instead, I rested my head on his shoulder and when he used his free hand to lightly touch my braids, I felt moisture start to pool in my vagina.

"We should walk the rest of the way. My GPS says it's like, less than a mile. You can get some pictures, GoGo." Clarke interrupted the moment.

"GoGo?" Northern repeated. "That your nickname?"

I nodded. "Yep. Just like the boots. I get called GoGo boots all of the time. And GoGo music."

He gave a small sympathetic smile. "What's your nickname, Clarke?"

Shrugging her shoulders, she responded. "Most people just call me 'Twin.'"

"Yeah, every set of twins I have ever known has been called 'Twin.' Is it weird? That people won't recognize your identity outside of being a twin?"

She considered him. "Well damn, Super Star. You're good looking and educated, huh? I don't think I've ever been asked that question. But yeah, it's annoying."

"I think it was more annoying when we were younger." I put in. "When we were trying to establish our own identities. Now, it doesn't bother me at all when people call me 'twin'." I cut my eyes at my sister. "Even Clarke calls me, 'Twin.' I just respond."

"I think it helps that we aren't identical. People don't just automatically assume that we're twins." Clarke narrowed her gaze at him. "Sometimes people come up to me and ask me to tell my "friend" that they think *she's* beautiful."

"Sorry Clarke. For the record, you're beautiful, too."

"Too late!" She said holding her hand to his face in fake anger. "My feelings are already hurt."

"Well, let me buy you dinner to make up for it." Northern suggested.

"Okay, if you insist."

"I do. I insist."

I let go of Northern's hand so he could fish some money out of his pocket to pay for the cab. Then the three of us exited and started walking towards the restaurant.

"Can you get a picture of us?" Clarke asked Northern, handing him her cell phone. She hugged me tightly, pulling our faces together.

I kissed her cinnamon colored cheek, as he snapped the picture.

It was a short walk to the restaurant. Less than a mile, like Clarke had estimated. Maybe five city blocks or so, but we managed to take a gang of pictures. Several of which featured Northern and me...and in all of them he was hugging me or touching me. Although the thought of a stranger touching me and/or hugging me would typically piss me off, it didn't with him. It didn't bother me at all. Honestly, I liked it.

Right before we got to the restaurant, I hopped on Northern's back. He didn't seem shocked or put out by my behavior. He held me up and waited patiently for Clarke to snap a picture.

Before I slid down off of his back, I pressed a gentle kiss to his chocolatey cheek. Once my feet were on the ground, he pulled me into a hug, and rested his chin on top of my head. I could've stayed right there, wrapped up in his arms, listening to his heart beat, smelling whatever delectable ass cologne he was wearing for hours.

He broke the hug, and the three of us entered the restaurant.

"Is it okay with you if these pictures end up on social media?" I asked, as we waited to be seated.

He seemed to consider the question. "Like on regular social media?" He lowered his voice. "Not like on the dark web, right?

Not like on porn sites or fetish sites for people who get turned on by piggyback rides, right?"

Clarke screamed in laughter, then clasped her hand over her own mouth. "Wow, Northern."

I chuckled, too. "No, not on the 'dark web.' On my own social media sites." I assured him.

"Like Instagram and Snapchat, right?"

I nodded, while I edited some pictures on my phone. "Yeah."

"Yeah, that's cool." He assured me.

"What do you do, Super Star?" Clarke asked, taking a bite of her scallop. "You said that fashion week is always work for you. What do you do?"

"I work in...music production." Northern responded, not bothering to move his hand from where it rested comfortably on my thigh. "Behind the scenes. I handled the music for the

Caprice SKR fashion show. My team and I make sure that the musical portion of the show goes off without a hitch. What about you? What do you do, Clarke?"

"I'm a NICU nurse. Newborn intensive care."

He looked impressed with her. I didn't blame him. She was impressive.

"Word?" He asked. "Check you out."

I felt anxiety start bubbling up in my stomach. I hated telling people what I did for a living. Typically, people acted like it wasn't a real job and I wasn't up for justifying myself to anybody, not even sexy ass Northern.

"What do you do, Indigo?"

I gave him my standard answer. "Marketing. Social media stuff. Brand management." I said vaguely.

He didn't push. He just squeezed my thigh, and sent a cascade of wetness into my already damp panties.

When we got back to the hotel, Clarke begged off having a drink with us at the hotel bar. She claimed that she needed to pack for our flight home the next morning, but I knew she was trying to give me some alone time with dude. My sister knew me better than anybody on earth, she knew I was vibing Northern.

I gave her a brief hug, before watching her walk away. Northern took my hand, which had somehow become the norm, considering he had been touching me all night - his hand on my thigh under the table at the restaurant. His fingers slowly moving through my braids in the taxi cab. Him pulling me close and hugging me tightly on the walk to the restaurant. Holding my hand while we walked through the hotel lobby. He was just touchy-feely and I liked it.

And even though he had been touching me all night long, electricity still shot from my hand directly to my vagina at the contact. I actually stutter-stepped as I walked, but he didn't seem to notice. Just like Clarke had said to me in French earlier, I was creaming my panties for dude.

I wasn't surprised when he bypassed the hotel bar, and ushered me to the bank of elevators that led to the hotel rooms upstairs. Positioning me against the wall, he covered my body with his, leaning down to whisper in my ear.

"Is it okay if we skip the bar, and have drinks in my room?"

I looked up at him. "Is it okay if we skip the drinks when we get to your room?"

CHAPTER TWO

Northern

Is it okay if we skip the drinks when we get to your room? *This girl.*

I managed to keep my hands mostly to myself in the elevator. I'm saying, I held Indigo in my arms, and pressed my pelvis into her ass, so that she could feel the physical evidence of what her mere presence was doing to me. I didn't however, cup her breasts or run my fingers over her nipples, like I was dying to do. I didn't unfasten her pants, and stick my hand into her panties on a search for her clit. I was actually quite proud of myself for the level of restraint I was showing. It was the least I could do, though. Because in all honesty, I really didn't plan on showing any restraint once I got her in my hotel room. I had been touching and teasing her all night, hell, I was ready to have her.

Sliding the key card into the slot, I unlocked the door. It had barely closed before I reached for Indigo. I almost smiled when I realized that she was reaching for me, too.

I bent to kiss her, invading her mouth and using my tongue to stroke hers. It felt like she almost melted against me and that made my dick get even harder, which I hadn't thought was possible. *This girl.*

Ever since I'd laid eyes on her in the hotel lobby, all I could think about was getting her alone. Now, we were alone. I pushed her jacket off of her shoulders. She helped, shimmying slightly and letting both her jacket and purse fall to the floor. Then my hands were on the button of the slacks she was wearing. I needed to free her blouse from the waistband of her pants, so that I could push it up and get to her breasts. I needed to get to her breasts.

It was while I was making quick work of her zipper that I noticed her hands were on my belt buckle. I smiled to myself. I liked this girl.

"You need help?" I questioned.

"Nah." Her voice was husky. "You just keep doing what you're doing, Super Star."

I pushed up her blouse. Her hands came off my waistband, and lifted into the air while I took off her shirt and tossed it into the darkness. Popping the clasp on her bra, I received my reward as her full breasts poured into my waiting hands.

Indigo struck gold right after me. I felt her warm, soft hands slide into my boxer briefs, then wrap around my dick.

“Uhm.” She said softly, mostly to herself.

“You worried?” I asked her. I’m not a braggart, or a particularly cocky dude, but I do know that I have a sizable dick. It was night time, the room was dark. I couldn’t see her face - couldn’t tell what she was thinking. “I’m gonna be gentle.” I assured her.

She didn’t respond.

“You need to slow down?” I offered, honestly hoping that she didn’t, but knowing that I needed to give her an out.

“We’re good. Just be gentle.” She said, leaning in and kissing my mouth roughly while simultaneously freeing my dick from my underwear.

I broke the kiss, dipped my head down and took her right nipple into my mouth. I savored it. She smelled so fucking good. Like fresh air, with a hint of delicate powder. Indigo moaned for me. I sucked harder on her nipple, then switched from the right to the left one.

While her head was thrown back, moans of pleasure escaping her lips, I pushed her pants and panties over her ass and hips. She helped, moving them down her legs, while I pulled my shirt off. After grabbing a condom from my wallet, I stepped out of my pants, leaving them in a heap in the middle of the floor.

Our bodies collided, flesh on flesh. I lowered my head claiming her mouth, deepening the kiss as I moved us towards the bed. I tossed the condom onto the mattress, hoping I would be able to find it when I needed it. Her juicy ass settled perfectly in my palms, as she wrapped her legs around me, firmly cementing my dick between the two of us.

"What are we waiting on?" She asked.

Fighting back the grin that threatened to overtake my face, I answered while laying her back on the bed. "Be patient." I positioned myself between her thighs and teased her, gently rubbing the head of my dick against her swollen clit while she whined and whimpered in response. I liked the way she sounded, so I kept up the rubbing. Not only were her moans sexy as hell, the increase in wetness that I felt against the tip of my dick made my balls strain in gratification.

The teasing went on and on, with me sliding right up to Indigo's opening, simulating the penetration that she wanted, pulling back at the last second. When Indigo's hips started to follow my dick and press towards the head, like she was trying to insert it herself, I knew it was time to give us both what we wanted.

"Please, Northern. Please." She begged.

It was the sexiest thing I thought I had ever heard. I quickly ripped the condom open and rolled it on. I promised her gentle, so I entered her body slowly giving her time to acclimate to my size.

"Damn," I said appreciatively in her ear. "You're tight as hell."

Indigo just moaned in response.

With her braids fanned out over the pillow, I couldn't help reaching out and grabbing a handful. I gave them a firm tug on the upstroke causing her eyes to fly open and grab my gaze.

"Yes." She encouraged me, her eyes boring into mine. "Yes."

So, I pulled her hair harder, and stroked her more deeply. "Damn, Girl! What the fuck are you trying to do to me?" She was contracting and pulsing like crazy, squeezing my dick to the rhythm of her own heartbeat.

Gripping the sheets, she cried my name like a prayer. "Northern. Oh my God, Northern. You feel so fucking good."

I put my mouth on her shoulder, biting down while she raised her hips and bucked the pussy up at me.

"Oh, you like that, huh?" I managed to tease even through the intense pleasure.

"I like it all." She confirmed breathily. "Please don't stop."

Why did she say that? Didn't she know how I ***had*** to respond to that? I lifted her right leg, and placed it over my shoulder. Then I flipped the fuck out, and giving the beautiful woman beneath me an orgasm became my only purpose in life.

My body slapped against hers, the bed bouncing, Indigo moaning and humming my name. Her volume and intensity rose until I knew she was on the verge of exploding.

Just when I was positive that I couldn't hold back any longer, she shrieked, wrapping her free leg around my waist. She pressed her pelvis up against me swallowing the entire shaft of my dick, trembling and with her breath coming out in short puffs, she came against me, coating me in thick, intoxicating creaminess. While aftershocks ripped through her quaking body, she milked me until I released my load, sending streams of hot semen shooting from my body.

When the involuntary jerking ceased and the tingles finally subsided, I pulled out of her, falling onto the bed. I gathered her into my arms, pulled her close and held her.

"Damn."

"Definitely, damn." She agreed.

Pulling her even closer, I kissed her on the cheek, reveling in the feeling of her body pressed up against mine. After a few moments, I released her from my embrace and made my way to the bathroom to dispose of the condom. When I came out, she was standing beside the bed, still nude. Even though I had just cum, my dick jumped at the sight of her.

"I've gotta go."

I nodded in understanding. "You've gotta pack."

She walked over to me, wrapped her arms around my waist, and rested her head in my chest. "You really are a beautiful man, Northern."

I kissed the top of her head. "Thanks. Take care of yourself, Indigo."

She went up on her tip-toes, pressed her lips to mine and kissed me gently. "You, too."

I watched in silence as she gathered her clothes, dressed, and walked out of my hotel room.

CHAPTER THREE

Indigo

The Friday night after I returned from Paris, I sat in front of my computer with my legs folded underneath me. Absent-mindedly, I played with my individual box braids as I scrolled through the pictures from my trip. There were a lot of pictures. Not to mention that Clarke had sent me the pictures she had taken, as well. As far as I was concerned, more was more. There was no such thing as having too many pictures. I needed to make sure that I was able to tell my "Paris Fashion Week" story the way that I wanted to tell it.

While there were well over three hundred photos to choose

from, my favorite shots were the eight pictures that featured Northern. My particular favorite was the one of me riding on his back. Seriously, I didn't know what possessed me to get on that man's back like that. Even Clarke reprimanded me about "just jumping on some random dude's back." I didn't care what Clarke was talking about. I knew what felt right to me. Northern...and me on his back felt right to me. Plus, the picture was fire. It was definitely in the top five of all of the pictures.

Honestly though, I wasn't the type to go around jumping on dude's backs. I'm a curvy girl. I wear a size 12, all day long. I've never had a complex about my weight, but I am realistic about it. I'm not as light as a feather or anything. Still, Northern didn't seem to mind my curves or my weight, at all. Not on his back, or in his bed.

I smiled at a different picture of Northern and me. He stood behind me with his arms around my waist, his chin almost touching my shoulder. We were both laughing at something Clarke said before she snapped the pic. I didn't remember what it was, but I remembered that Northern was slow to release me after the picture. Ooh, and he dragged his lips across my neck as he pulled away. The sensation made my nipples come to life. His lips were so soft, and his breath was so warm. Yeah, that was a good memory. It was also the precise moment that I decided that I was smashing dude if the opportunity presented itself.

I logged onto Instagram and posted the picture of the moment that made me give Northern the coochie, as well as several others, taking care to make sure that my pictures told the visual story of my time in France. Finally, I moved on to my YouTube channel.

My notifications pinged. Then pinged again. And pinged once more.

Damn. I thought to myself. The pictures were fire, but damn. My notifications pinged again. Then pinged again.

I minimized YouTube, and quickly brought up my Instastories. There were over 50 comments.

"Uhm." I said thoughtfully. "Must be a quiet day on Instagram."

Then I scrolled down to the comments and started to read.

"Let me find out that @GoGoGoesGlam is getting horsey-back rides from @NorthernKin."

"@GoGoGoesGlam and @NorthernKin cute together."

"Some bitches have all the luck. @GoGoGoesGlam booed up with @NorthernKin."

"Chocolate and vanilla. Uhm uhm good. @GoGoGoesGlam and @NorthernKin."

Who is Northern, that people would be so riled up to see him on my Instagram? I wondered. Maybe he *actually* was an influencer.

Northern Kin. I repeated to myself. I knew his name should mean something to me. It was obvious, by how my followers were reacting to him, and the fact that they were tagging him in my post - but I was drawing a complete blank. I didn't know Northern as anybody except the gorgeous dude who had fucked me well and wouldn't get out of my head.

So, I did what I felt anybody in my position would do. I slid into his DMs.

"So, who are you really, @NorthernKin?" I wrote.

While I waited for him to respond, I hopped on google, and searched the term, "Northern Kin."

The first thing that came up was for something called "Northern Kin Productions." I clicked the link. Sure enough, Northern's face popped up. I clicked through the tabs, viewing picture after picture of Northern with famous musical artists. Northern with Trey Whisper. Northern with Licks Harlowe. Northern with Tahkim Steele. And the millisecond before I clicked on a photo of him with Joya Bingham-Payne and KJ Jamison, I knew exactly who he was.

Clarke and I were away at college when our cousin, Joya Bingham-Payne started to embark on a music career. I remembered Joya touring the country with KJ Jamison for a little while when KJ was a brand new artist. The two of them had recorded a successful single on *Ride or Die Records*. Joya was even offered a record deal, based on that success, but she found out that she was pregnant by Nasir Payne before she could sign, and her life had gone in a different direction.

Northern McKinley produced that single. He produced my cousin's highly successful single. Actually, he had produced hundreds of successful singles. He'd won Grammys, Billboard Awards, American Music Awards, BET Awards, and so on. Still, I hadn't recognized him or his name. And neither had Clarke. I couldn't understand how I didn't recognize him. I could only blame it on the phenomenon of the deep, dark chocolate. Maybe I was distracted by the fact that he was so gorgeous, and so humble, and so down-to-earth. What millionaire music producer hung out with twins as crazy as me and my sister just on G.P.?

My notifications pinged. There was a response to my DM.

Send me your phone number, Indigo. The message read.

Well, okay then. I thought to myself, as I quickly typed my phone number into the little box and waited.

A few moments later, my phone rang, and butterflies took off inside my stomach. Right before I worked myself up, I had a quick little conversation with myself. "Listen, GoGo, chill the hell out. You got this." Then I answered my phone. "Hey."

"Hey yourself. What's up? How're you doing?"

His voice was exactly the same. Still velvety, deep and sexy.

"I don't know, yet." I said honestly. "Did I mess up?"

"What makes you feel like you might've messed up?"

"Uhm, maybe the fact that as soon as I posted those pictures, I broke the internet. I'm saying, my followers went crazy. They tagged you like, a million times."

"Yeah. They did." He agreed good-naturedly.

"Sorry." I told him. "If you had just told me who you are, I never would've posted the pictures. Especially the one of me on your back. You're a world-renowned music producer, and I'm riding on your back, like you're some regular Stan. Ugh! That is not okay."

He laughed and I could just imagine those deep dimples etched into his cheeks.

"You're good, Sweetheart. I don't have a problem with the fact that you posted that picture. You asked me if I was okay with you putting my pictures on social media and I signed off on it. Granted, I didn't realize at the time that you were "GoGo-GoesGlam," some type of fucking beauty guru. Now, I've been tagged about a hundred thousand times. You're over there making me relevant again, and shit."

I laughed.

"And as far as you treating me like a Stan, I was definitely Stanning you, Indigo. You're beautiful."

"Why didn't you tell me who you are?"

"I did. I told you that I'm Northern. That's who I am. Regardless of whatever social media or the internet is trying to tell you about who I am, I'm Northern. You of all people should get that, Indigo. Are you who social media and the internet say you are?"

He had a point. "I should have told you that I'm an influencer when I asked you if I could post your pictures. I apologize for that."

"It's cool. I don't think you telling me would've made much of a difference. I don't think I would've understood your reach, even if you would've told me. You've got like...millions of followers, girl. Clearly, you're a celebrity in your own right."

"I'm only Instagram famous." I assured him, then quickly changed the subject. "You're from Chicago?"

"Yeah." He said slowly. "That's like a weird coincidence, huh?"

"Yeah. I went all the way to Paris to have a one night stand with somebody who lives up the street."

"I've seen crazier shit happen."

"Really? Because I haven't."

The line was quiet for a moment. Finally, Northern broke the silence.

"I can't stop thinking about you."

"Get outta my head. I'm having the same issue." I replied. Butterflies fluttered in my stomach.

"Why didn't we exchange information?"

"It was supposed to be a one-time thing, Northern. A Paris

fling."

"Who the hell decided that?"

"We both did." I confirmed with a smile on my lips, although he couldn't see me.

"I didn't agree to that. I wanna see you, again. And again. Then some more."

I laughed. "Is that really a good idea? I mean, you're just going to become more obsessed, the more time you spend with me." I teased.

"Counting on it."

I liked his confidence. "Well, I'm right here. If you wanna see me, come and get me. Or tell me where you wanna meet." I paused. "I mean, if you're even in Chicago. You're famous and all, you might live in L.A. or something."

"Actually, I live in Atlanta." He told me.

"Buckhead?" I teased.

"How'd you know? Is that where the famous influencers stay?"

"The ones from Atlanta." I confirmed. "Are you in Atlanta?"

"I'm in Chicago. You up for having company?"

"If that company is you? Yep."

Northern chuckled. I smiled to myself.

"Send me your address."

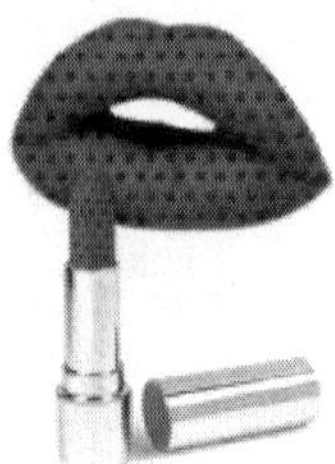

I moved around my apartment as quickly as I could. I tended to keep a tidy place, plus I had a housekeeper that came every Monday. Still, I ran the vacuum over my area rug, fluffed up the pillows on my sofa and lit all of the candles that were scattered around my combined living room/dining room. I loaded my dishwasher. Changed the linen on my bed, and lit candles in there, as well. I quickly spruced up the guest bath. Then, as an afterthought, I spruced up my master bathroom.

I gargled some mouthwash, and changed into a matching panty and bra set, that was appropriate for "company." After throwing on leggings and a t-shirt that said something about celebrating melanin in all shades, I went into my office, sat down at my computer, and tried to do some editing work before Northern arrived.

When I couldn't get my brain to focus on editing, I turned

off the computer, left the office, and went into the living room. I plopped down on the sofa, turning on the television and flipping aimlessly through channel after channel.

When my phone vibrated in my hand a few minutes later, I really hoped it was Northern telling me that he was on his way. I read the text.

Northern: ***I'm outside your door. Come let me in.***

His text surprised me, because I lived in a secure building with a doorman. That doorman was supposed to call up to me, and let me know any and every time I had a visitor. Clearly, the doorman was fan-girling over Northern or slacking or something.

Nevertheless, I walked over to the door, looked out of the peephole, and there he was, standing in my hallway. I unlocked the door, and opened it.

"Hey. Come on in." I said, as coolly as I could. He was still as gorgeous as I remembered him. His skin was still as chocolatey. His eyes were still arresting when they were trained on me, like they were now.

And even though I had moved to the side to allow him to enter into my place, Northern still brushed his body against mine as he moved past me. My nipples didn't have any sense of decorum, they just went ahead and stood at attention merely from the contact of his body against mine.

I turned my back to him, so I could lock the door, as well as get control of my traitorous body. He didn't play fair, though, because he came behind me and kissed me gently on the neck. Heat radiated through my entire being. His lips were my weakness.

When I felt like I could face him without melting into a sloppy puddle right in my own foyer, I turned around. Before I could move, or get a word out of my mouth, he backed me up against the door. I watched frozen in place, as he dipped his head down and captured my mouth, softly kissing my lips. While I was still floating from that sensation, he kissed me for real, plunging his tongue into my mouth, and slowly coaxing me to let myself go. It didn't take much to convince me to match his passion. I had been fantasizing about kissing him since I walked out of his hotel room in Paris. I moaned in contentment while Northern devoured my mouth. Right when I was ready to drop my panties, he finally released me from his spell.

"What's up, GoGoGoesGlam?"

I shook my head, as much to clear the fog that he had left, as to answer his question. "Not much." I took a beat. "Uhm, how did you get up here without the doorman calling up to me?"

He graced me with his dimpled smile. "Look, I know that you and your sister don't know who I am, but this is my town. I always get recognized at home. Everybody in Chicago went to high school with me, kindergarten with me. Babysat me. Grew up on the block with me. Everybody knows me. So, they treat me like fam."

I narrowed my eyes at him. "So, my doorman treated you like fam, rather than protect me from a possible intruder? That's kinda messed up. I might have to report him." I teased.

He kissed me on the lips, again. "It's cool. He actually did go to high school with me. So, you don't have to report him."

At first I couldn't tell if he was being serious or not, but I realized he was joking when he winked at me.

He took in my place, as I led him beyond the foyer. He spotted the "studio" set-up inside my office.

"What were you doing? You working on your social media?"

I shook my head. "I tried, but I couldn't concentrate."

"You couldn't concentrate? Am I taking credit for that?"

"Yeah, you are."

"Yo, I can't say that I'm sorry about it. You've been messing up my concentration since Paris." He wrapped his arms around me and pulled me into yet another hug. It was obvious to me that Northern was the touchy-feely type. At least, he was always touching and feeling on me. I liked it.

I led him over to the sofa. When he sat down, I made myself comfortable on his lap.

"So, this is your seat of choice?" He asked me.

"As much as you've been touching on me, and kissing on me since you got here, you should know you're gonna have to put out before I let you leave. Why waste time pretending that it's not what it is?"

"Basically, I hugged you one too many times since I've been here, and now I'm getting fucked tonight?"

I shrugged my shoulders as I fought off a grin. "Pretty much."

"A'ight." He assented as he adjusted me, so that we were both comfortable. Then he pushed my braids to the side, and nipped at my neck. My neck was so sensitive. It took a gang of self-control not to moan at the conflicting sensations of pleasure and pain, but there wasn't a damn thing I could do about the wetness pooling in my center.

"Northern, before it goes down," I began.

"Uh huhm." He nipped my neck, again, sending a tiny shiver of pain through me, which he soothed by sucking lightly.

"Stop before you mark me." I protested weakly.

"Oh, I'm gonna mark you, Indigo." He assured, before kissing the spot again. "Before it goes down, what?"

"Before it goes down, I need to tell you where I stand."

His face got serious, even though desire still blazed in his chocolate brown eyes. "Where do you stand, Indigo?"

"I want to play with you, but I'm not looking to get serious."

"Okay." He said thoughtfully. "So, you wanna get together

and fuck, but that's as far as you want it to go? I'm not judging. I'm just asking for clarity."

"I get it." I assured him, with a nod. "I'm saying that I'm not expecting this to turn into a relationship or anything."

He was quiet, so I kept my mouth shut, too. But then, the silence got uncomfortable.

"What're you thinking, Northern?" I asked, as I started to stand up from his lap.

He held me tightly. "A couple of things." He settled me back into his lap.

"Like what?" I prompted.

He scrubbed his hand over his handsome face, giving his beard a light scratch. "First, I'm thinking that every time a woman has ever said that to me in my life, she's never been able to follow through. It always ends up getting complicated. Expectations end up being different for both people. Feelings end up getting hurt."

"How many times have women said that to you, Northern?"

"Enough." He admitted. "And it always ends badly."

I knew that it was a widely held belief that women had a harder time compartmentalizing sex than men did. I knew that women sometimes agreed to "relationship" terms that weren't really in their best interest, hoping that things would work out their way in the end. This wasn't that.

"I can't speak for them." I said finally. "I can only speak for myself. Right now, today…I just wanna play. If that changes, I'll come to you and tell you what's up. We can reestablish expectations, or decide to stop being 'playmates'."

"Playmates." He repeated with a chuckle, as he ran his hand over my thigh. "Cute."

"What else are you thinking?"

"I'm thinking that I must be the rebound guy."

"What makes you think that?"

"The way you're coming at this. Like you're working out the terms of a business deal." He held up his hand to stop me from interrupting him. "Transparency. That's all I'm looking for, Indigo." He hugged me tightly, tugged my braids playfully, then moved me off of his lap, so that I was sitting next to him. "You're distracting as hell. I need to focus while we discuss this."

Instantaneously I felt the absence of his warmth. I wanted to climb back into his lap, but I didn't. He was right. We both needed to focus.

"Am I the rebound guy?"

I really didn't want to get into all of that right before I was trying to get it to go down. “Does it make a difference if you are?” I asked instead.

He didn’t hesitate. “Not in the way you’re probably thinking.”

“Well, you’re not the rebound guy. Not in the way *you’re* probably thinking.” I conceded. “Not in the ‘some dude played me out and left me heartbroken’ type way. More in the, ‘I found myself in the middle of a fucked up situation that I never saw coming, and my heart did take a little bit of a beating...but not nearly as much of a beating as my feelings took’.”

He eyed me. “Is it weird that those two things sound exactly the same to me?”

“Nah.” I shook my head. “Because you don’t know the story.”

“So, just sex? Convenient sex, when we happen to be in the same city and can get at each other?”

Hearing him say it aloud made me start to doubt myself. For a second, I wondered if I was one of those women who agreed to “relationship” terms that weren’t in my best interest.

I looked over at him, with his chocolatey skin, his deep dimples, his full lips, his brown eyes, his beard, and his easy smile - looking *exactly* like what I liked in a man and I knew that I was going to have to work hard as hell to keep things strictly physical.

“Let’s revisit it later.” I said, trying to buy myself some time.

Northern laughed loudly. "If that's what you wanna do, Baby Girl. I'mma let you make it. You run the show. But for the record, I'm feeling something like things are gonna end up getting real complicated."

I ignored his warning.

Northern said that he would let me run the show, but then he picked up the remote and killed the television. Then he stood up from the sofa, and took his phone out of his back pocket. I watched silently, as his fingers moved across the screen. Before I knew it, a familiar song floated out of his phone - "Groove With You." by The Isley Brothers.

"I'm a music guy." Northern explained with a shrug of his shoulders. "I like music."

He sat back down, grabbed me, and placed me on his lap facing him, so that my legs straddled his thighs. I wiggled around until I could feel the print of his dick right where I needed to feel it.

He took my face in his hands, and attached his lips to mine. His tongue found mine and caressed it gently. Northern was good at kissing. That was the only clear thought I could make. His kisses made my clit throb. After a few seconds of having him ravish my mouth, I could feel the level of moisture intensifying in my panties.

He palmed my ass while I pressed my pelvis into his dick, so that it was directly against my clit. I loved that sensation. It was the sweetest torture that I could imagine. His fingers found my nipples, and squeezed.

He let one hand slide inside the waistband of my leggings and into my panties. I was already soaking wet when his thumb claimed my swollen clit. He rubbed it gently, but consistently, until I found myself doing more moaning in Northern's mouth, than kissing.

He pulled his mouth away from mine, but kept up the assault on my clit.

Why is he so good at making me melt? I thought to myself.

"Where's the bedroom?" He asked me.

"In the back." I panted, barely able to get even the tiniest bit of control over myself.

He removed his hand from my panties, but seemed to realize that I was still dazed. He spoke to me in a gentle, but authoritative tone. "I'm gonna lift you up. Put your feet on the floor, Indigo."

Was it weird that I loved the way he said my full name? "Okay." I agreed, and placed my feet on the floor when he lifted me.

Northern stood up, placing a kiss on the top of my head. "Where's your bedroom?" He asked again.

I came back to myself. “This way.” I told him, and started to walk. I paused and as an afterthought added, “Uh, bring the music.”

The sounds of the Isley Brothers filled my bedroom. That paired with the candle light set a very seductive scene. I stood beside my bed while Northern stopped right inside my doorway, his eyes glued to me. I pulled my t-shirt over my head.

Walking closer, he moved over to my dresser. Leaning against it, he shook his head at me. “Slower, Ma. I’m not in a rush.”

I smiled at him. I hadn’t expected him to say that, but if he wanted me to go more slowly, I could do that.

“Come here.” He beckoned.

I walked over to him. He pulled me into his arms, running

his hands over my skin.

"You're so fucking soft." He said, nipping at my earlobe. His hands were still traveling over my back, and at my waist. "The things I could do to you."

"Do them." I said, without thinking. Then, I started to work on the front of his button up.

He unclasped my bra, and let it drop to the floor. I finally got his shirt unbuttoned and pushed it down off of his broad shoulders. I could not hold back my disappointment when I was confronted with his wife beater.

I sighed. "Why do you have on so many clothes?"

He released me, pulling the offending garment over his head and flinging it to the floor. "You're kinda impatient, huh?"

"I just want what I want when I want it." My hands moved over his muscular chest, rubbing across his tattooed skin.

"Oh yeah?" He backed me up towards the bed.

"Don't you?" I whispered, attacking the fly of his jeans.

"I do. But sometimes," he paused to take my left nipple into his mouth and suck it.

I arched into him, enjoying the tingles that were coursing through me.

"Sometimes," he released my nipple, "the anticipation heightens the sensations. Lose the leggings."

While I shimmied out of my leggings, he took off his jeans. I put my hands inside the waistband of my panties.

Northern placed his large hands on top of mine. "Anticipation, Baby. Get on the bed."

Reluctantly, I left my panties on and climbed into the bed. Northern climbed in beside me, pulling my body to his. My breasts flattened against his hard pectoral muscles when our lips met in a soul stirring kiss. He ran his hands over the curve of my ass, touching everything he wanted to touch, before sliding a hand inside my panties. I parted my legs instinctively and Northern's fingers found my slick, wet center. I moaned when his finger slipped inside me, pushing myself down against it. I should have been embarrassed by how wet I was, but I wasn't. Apparently my vagina was well aware that "daddy" was home.

Northern kissed me possessively, his mouth warm and wet and sweet like peppermint. He was a hair puller, too. Tugging my braids as his mouth took me places that were beautiful, and serene making my stomach do flip-flops - making me drippy and even wetter.

He removed his hand from my panties as his lips left my mouth and found my neck. Dropping kisses and nipping me as he went down my body. His lips traveled south and kissed and nipped my breasts.

He continued downward, kissing my stomach and belly button before spreading my legs wide, settling between them, and hovering over my vagina. Our eyes met and the desire I was feeling was mirrored back at me.

CHAPTER 4

Northern

Indigo was sexy as hell. The way she was looking at me, with fire blazing in her eyes made my already hard dick brick up even more. It took every ounce of self-control I had, not to rip the panties from her ass and dive into the pussy. Instead, I slowed myself down, and placed a kiss in her middle. Her panties were wet against my mouth, but I already knew that they would be. I kissed her pussy, again - inhaling the scent of her. The muskiness of her made my mouth water a little bit. Sliding her panties down, she lifted her hips for me.

She had the prettiest pussy. It was bare of hair, except for a mound right in the middle that looked like it was in the shape of a heart. I smiled to myself before I dug in, giving her a long, slow lick. The next lick was decidedly harder. I felt her hands come around the sides of my head.

"Yes, Northern." She moaned.

She was demonstrative during sex and I was totally with that. I liked the way she sounded. Her moans, shouts and whimpers just added more fuel to the fire that was already raging inside me.

I put my entire tongue up against her opening. Made it vibrate right there, and let her delicious creaminess spill easily into my mouth. She tasted like salt, honey, and some type of deliciousness that I didn't have the vocabulary to describe. I could've stayed there all night, but it wasn't all about me. It was about her, and her pleasure. I captured her clit between my lips, and sucked it hard, letting my teeth gently knock against it every so often. She was thrashing underneath me like crazy, but I didn't let up. Actually, I started to tease her, removing my mouth to speak.

"You trying to wake up your whole building?"

She wailed in response.

Flipping her over, I put her up on all fours. I slid underneath her on my back and brought her hips down so her pussy could rest firmly in my mouth. Then I licked.

"Oh my God!!!!" She sounded good as hell to me whining loudly.

So, I went for broke and put in work. She rewarded me by dripping ounces of sweet honey into my mouth that I could've swallowed by the bucket. When she came, moaning, and writhing on top of me, I lapped up her juices.

She fell off of me, curled into a ball, and tried to collect herself. I used that time to grab a condom from the pocket of my jeans, and protect us.

"You okay?" I asked her.

She looked over at me. Her face was flushed pink, but she looked happy. "Yeah."

"Good." I told her. Then, I pulled her back up on all fours, and I went in from behind. She shivered in response, like she was still tingling.

"Damn, if you could feel what I'm feeling." I told her. Her pussy was scorching hot. And the way it was squeezing me, made me feel like I had my dick in a vise grip.

She didn't respond verbally, she just hummed happily and pushed her ass into me roughly.

We had only been together once before, so I didn't know her body well enough to know her limits. I didn't want to hurt her, so I was gentle with my strokes even though I really wanted to bang her out. It was apparent that she had other ideas in mind, though. She was throwing the ass back at me, like she wanted it harder. I took my cue from her and picked up the speed and the force. Reaching around her body, I took her full breasts into my hands and held them as I pumped her, periodically squeezing her nipples as hard as I could.

She moaned and groaned loudly, her middle so over saturated and juicy that I could hardly stay inside.

"Why are you so wet?" I asked, as I pumped her with strokes I pulled up from the floorboards.

"Because you feel so good." She responded breathlessly. "Ooooooooohhhhhhh! I'm about to cum, Boo. Please let me cum." She begged sexily.

Shit. I didn't get how she managed to sound innocent, but erotic at the same damn time. I placed my hands on her hips, holding her still while I plowed into her harder. I felt her pussy expand around my dick and suck me in deeper. I moaned involuntarily, my eyes rolling back in my head momentarily.

"You feel so good." I said softly, then I let go of her right breast, my fingers finding her throbbing clit. I rubbed it steadily, while she noisily expressed her pleasure. When I pinched it, she screamed out, starting to squirm, while her pussy clamped around my dick. I felt my orgasm start to build like a ball of fire in my lower stomach. The pleasure was almost too intense to handle. I plunged in over and over, so hard that the room around me became a blur. There was just Indigo and Northern. Nothing else existed. Then the explosion came, and jets of cum shot from my body. She was in the middle of her own thunderstorm, but I couldn't help holding her still while my balls drained themselves.

After what felt like an eternity, I finally eased out of her. She fell flat against the bed, and lay there motionless. I smiled in the darkness.

"Damn, you're good in bed."

"Right back at you." She managed.

"Where's the bathroom, Gorgeous?" I was still trying to catch my breath.

She gestured to a doorway on the other side of the bedroom. Crossing the room, I stepped into her bathroom. I wrapped the condom up in toilet paper, dropped it in the trashcan, took a piss and flushed. After I washed and dried my hands, I grabbed one of the washcloths she had hanging in there as decoration. I ran it under warm water, and left the bathroom.

She was still laying in the same exact spot that I left her. I gently wiped between her legs with the washcloth, and cleaned up the mess that the two of us had made. Then, I took the washcloth back in the bathroom and set it on the counter.

Sliding back into the bed next to her, I pulled her naked body to mine. She curled into me while I absentmindedly ran my hand over the curve of her left hip. I couldn't seem to resist touching Indigo. Her skin was just...silky. I liked the feel of it. If I was keeping it completely 100% with myself, I liked Indigo more than I would've expected to.

Even though I found success in an industry that was at its very core, misogynistic, hedonistic, sexist, and anti-relationship, I didn't let that shit corrupt my general character.

I grew up watching men love on women. My grandfather was one of my biggest idols as a kid. He was a good dude. Upstanding, hard-working, smart, honest, and cool as hell. He had this habit of constantly feeling my grandmother up in front of me. That shit was disturbing as hell to me as a kid, but then later on in life...I got it. He was always grabbing my grandmother around her waist, and hugging her tightly. Whenever he would catch me watching them, he would wink at me and say in a barely audible voice, "soft."

I think seeing that conditioned me to always associate women with being soft. When I interacted with the "fairer sex", I didn't see bitches or hoes. I just saw "soft." Even if the chick in question was acting bitchy. Even if she was hard as hell. Even if she approached me with her figurative or literal dukes up. Even if she was the type to never crack a smile. I just basically saw "soft." I liked "soft." Who the hell didn't?

My father was another idol of mine. He was a military dude. A naval officer who worked out of the Naval Station at Great Lakes. He was strict and regimented as hell, but he loved his family. He spent his time at home loving on my mother, and spoiling my three sisters and me.

My father was the type that liked to laugh, and joke around. For some reason he thought of himself as a comedian. Probably because my mother encouraged him, with her laughter and shit. He was corny as hell, but he could always get my mom to smile for him. I got to grow up watching my parents be friends. It was obvious to anybody who met them that they genuinely liked each other. Being so up-close-and-personal to their relationship, I learned that women weren't my opponents. They weren't the enemy. My father always treated my mother like his teammate. When he won, she won, and vice versa. I knew for a fact that women could be valued teammates. So, whatever dumb ass, women-hating shit 90% of the dudes in hip hop (or music in general) were on, I wasn't with it.

I wasn't looking for a teammate, though. Mainly, I was just looking to chill. I had spent years in the industry "running the streets", as my mother called it. When she said it, she basically meant whoring around with different chicks. I didn't consider myself a "man-whore", but I couldn't lie - I definitely liked pussy. And I had definitely whored around in more than my fair share of pussy in my day. But the level of energy that it took to maintain that lifestyle in this day and age was exhausting. Or maybe I was just getting old as hell. Plus, I did not want to end up as that too old motherfucker that still frequents the club, hitting on chicks younger than my nieces. That shit was pathetic and sad.

I just wanted to chill. What did that look like? Hell if I knew.

I looked down at Indigo. Her eyes were shut. I didn't think she was asleep, but she looked like she was. Her face was turned towards me and her lips were arranged in a pretty pout. I leaned over and kissed her. When I did it a second time, she kissed me back.

"Do you need to go?" She asked, her eyes still closed.

I wasn't necessarily the "cuddling type", but I also wasn't the type to get his shot, then hit the door. Besides, we had done the "fuck and bounce out" thing in Paris. I had questions about her. The only way I knew to get answers was to talk to her.

"I'm good." I pulled her closer.

"What's your workout routine like, Northern? Your abs are flatter than a mug." Her eyes were low, but they were finally open.

I chuckled. She was wild. I did not expect her to say that. "Six days a week I run and I lift. Three days a week, I concentrate solely on my core." I took a beat. "Why? You wanna work out with me?"

She winked a lazy eye at me. "I just did. Unless you forgot."

I palmed her heavy ass. "Nah, I didn't forget."

She slid her hand between us, moving it farther and farther down, until she reached her destination. Yep. I was half hard. She held my dick tenderly in her grasp.

"When do you go back to Atlanta?" She slowly stroked

the tip.

Honestly, I found it somewhat challenging to answer the question when she did that, but I didn't want her to stop.

"Probably tomorrow."

"Do you travel a lot?"

"Nah. Not as much as I used to. I do fashion week in New York, and Paris and a few things in between. Otherwise, I just kinda chill." I took a breath. "I spend as much time as possible in South Carolina."

"South Carolina?" She repeated, her hand freezing mid-caress.

And I knew what was coming next. Anytime I told somebody that I spent my free time in South Carolina, they always asked some variant of the same question. *"What's in South Carolina?"*

Not Indigo, though.

"I love South Carolina." She stated dreamily. "My parents have a little beach bungalow on Isle of Palms. That's where we spent all of our vacations growing up. You have artists in South Carolina?"

"Not at all. South Carolina isn't about music for me. It's about peace of mind. And what I'm doing next, when I leave music in the rear view mirror."

She let her hand resume working it's magic. I was fully hard now.

"Do you have an end-game?" I asked, gesturing toward my brick-hard dick.

"I do." She assured me, then slid down my body. When she was perched directly over my dick, with her lips parted sexily, she trained her gaze on me. Our eyes met. "Fair warning, I am not a professional."

"Duly noted." I assured her.

With that, the swollen head of my dick disappeared into Indigo's wet, hot mouth. She sucked hard, making a tight ring with her lips.

I had a nefarious sexual past. And in the past, I'd had a lot of women do a lot of freaky, kinky things to me. Indigo didn't have their level of experience. But she was...Indigo and as far as my dick was concerned, that seemed to be enough. She stroked the sensitive underside with her tongue, and sent a shiver through my body causing my hips to lift off the bed a little bit. She slid her hand over the lower shaft, and jerked me while she sucked. It felt good as hell.

She doesn't give herself enough credit, I thought to myself as my eyes drifted shut.

She pulled back, ran her tongue across the tip, then took me into her mouth as deeply as she could. I tugged on her braids, and pushed her head down even further. She let me, humming sexily while she sucked me. The vibrations sent tremors through my entire body.

After a few minutes of intense pleasure, I knew I was on the verge. "Nah. I need you. Now." I said, pulling my dick from her sweet mouth.

I grabbed my jeans, and rifled through the pocket for another condom. Once I found it, I sheathed myself.

She lay back, her legs falling open. I pushed them open wider still, and slid easily inside. She felt *so* good. Her middle was hotter than an inferno, and deep, like it was bottomless. I gave her long strokes that drove her wild. Placing both hands in her hair, I pulled roughly. It was obvious that she liked that, too. Then I kissed her passionately. She whimpered and matched me stroke for stroke, bringing her hips up to meet mine in a perfect rhythm. I rode her waves for what seemed like an eternity.

When she started making the noises that let me know she was about to climax again, I picked up my intensity.

"Northern." She mumbled.

"Yeah, Gorgeous." I responded, pinning her arms to the bed over her head.

I buried my dick as deeply inside her as I could, and followed that by burying my face in the sweet curve of her neck. I think I came first, but she was so close behind me, that it was almost like we came together. I collapsed on top of her.

"Oh my God, Northern." She said, still panting.

Raising up on my forearms, I looked into her pretty face. "Hell, yeah, oh my God. Can I fucking keep you, Indigo?" I rolled off of her, laying next to her on my back.

"Probably. If you agree to hit it just like that everyday... yeah."

"I'll hit it however you want." I promised, gathering her into my arms.

I must have dozed off, because when I heard movement, I peeled open one eye, then the other. Indigo leaned over her dresser, blowing out a candle. She was still naked, and the sight of her silhouette made my dick jump.

"Stand down, dude." I said out loud.

She spun around quickly, giving me a small smile when our eyes met. "What'd you say?"

I sat up on my elbows. “I told my dick to ‘stand down.’ He was ready to come after you, again.”

“Why’re you stopping him?”

With a smirk, I replied. “It’s late. What time is it?” My phone was on her dresser, where I left it. It was still playing the Isley Brothers.

She tapped the button. “1:39.”

Stretching thoroughly, I swung my legs around to the floor.

“You’re a beautiful man, Northern McKinley.” She said watching me unabashedly.

“And you’re a beautiful woman, Indigo Cross. You sure I can’t put you in my luggage and take you back to Atlanta with me?”

“You leaving later today?”

“I am.”

“I gotta come to Atlanta to get my shots?”

I couldn’t tell if she was joking or not, so I played it through. “You down? Cuz I’ll buy you a plane ticket.”

“I’m down.” She assured me. “But I’ll buy my own plane ticket.”

I raised an eyebrow and asked, “you sure?”

“Yeah.” She nodded slowly. “Maybe I’m tripping, but something about you buying plane tickets for me to come sex you feels like hoe-ing.”

I held up my hands in a sign of surrender. “Ay, I’m not trying to do anything that makes you feel..."

"I know you're not. You didn't mean it that way. It's just me."

Standing up from the bed, I walked across the room towards her. When I was in front of her, I pulled her into my arms, once again ignoring the fact that my greedy-ass dick jumped at the mere touch of her.

"I wanna see you. I don't want distance to be a deterrent. So, I want you to know that I'm willing to do whatever it takes to make sure it isn't one. I'm willing to pay for the ability to spend time with you. I'm not willing to pay for your body, Sweetheart."

I stopped short of adding that I didn't pay for ass, figuring that was implied.

"I'll think about it."

I was easy in my response. "Good."

Later, after we were dressed, I had Indigo walk me to her front door. I turned to face her, before I exited.

"Listen, while we're doing this," I gestured between the two of us, "you're not seeing nobody else. This," I placed my hand between her legs, "belongs to me. I'm greedy, and I'm selfish. I suck at sharing."

"Ditto."

I gave her a nod. “Duly noted.”

She stood up on her tip-toes and leaned forward. I bent down and attached myself to her lush lips. Indigo’s kisses were fire. It was like she sent telepathy straight to my dick through them motherfuckers. When I was kissing her, it was like I could hear her thinking, “fuck me, Northern.”

I squeezed her firm ass, then broke the kiss.

“See you.” She said, looking up at me with heat still blazing in her pretty brown eyes.

I knew I had to get out of there, or I would never leave. Still, I couldn’t help running the pad of my thumb over her nipple one last time. “See you, Gorgeous.”

CHAPTER FIVE

Indigo

A week after my rendezvous with Northern, I hung out with my sister, and three of our cousins. We were at our cousin, Joya's house, helping her disassemble her nursery, so that she could move her youngest daughter, Lyric, into a "big girl" bedroom. I low-key figured that Joya was pregnant again, and wasn't ready to share, but it was whatever.

I sat on the floor, messing around with the pink wooden letters that spelled LYRIC - that I had taken off of the wall. In all honesty, I was sitting there feeling a way. I couldn't help but wonder why I was spending my weekend helping Joy dismantle her nursery, rather than spending it underneath Northern getting my back blown out.

"What's wrong, GoGo?" Joya asked me.

I guess my face and my demeanor gave me away. I looked up at her. Her eyes were full of concern. Joya was the oldest female cousin, which made her the "mother hen" of the Watson girls.

"Nothing." I told her. She was in love. Happy. Married. Settled. I didn't want to put my problems on her.

"GoGo's in love." Clarke teased.

I was surprised that my twin was so off base when it came to what I was thinking and/or feeling. I wasn't in love. I was sad and disappointed. I was horny, and missing my playmate. I was a lot of different things, in love wasn't one of them. I didn't bother contradicting her, though.

"With who?" My cousin, Mecca Goode asked.

"Northern McKinley." Joya stated.

I made eyes at her, wondering how she even knew about Northern and me.

She made eyes back at me. "What? I follow your Instagram...and his."

"You're dating gorgeous ass, Northern McKinley?" Mecca asked. "Go awf, little cous."

I didn't know why having to admit that we weren't actually dating made a pit form in my stomach. I ignored it, and answered her truthfully. "We aren't dating. We're having sex."

"Lucky girl." Joya said softly.

"Shut the hell up." Clarke told her. "Your man is the sexiest, finest, richest, most successful dude ever. You don't get to have him, and lust after Northern, too." She paused and teased. "With your pregnant ass."

Joya shook her head. "I am not pregnant. It's just time to move Lyric outta this nursery. Stop starting rumors."

"Whatever." Clarke said.

"Anyway, Nasir *is* gorgeous, and sexy and rich and successful. But that does not negate Northern's fineness." Joya told her.

"Not at all." My cousin Kyndall Rivers agreed. "All that chocolate wrapped up with a handsome face, and that body. And you get to have that pressed up against you, GoGo? I'm jealous as hell. And I know he's a beast in bed." She paused. "Is that why you're in love? Because the dick is outstanding?"

"I'm not in love." I protested. I wasn't in love. I mean, I liked Northern. I thought he was gorgeous and sexy and had me sprung on the sex. I couldn't stop thinking about him and missed him like crazy. I definitely wanted him to hit this again and I got butterflies from his text messages, and phone calls. Still, I didn't love him. More like, "lusted him."

"Limerence." Joya said, folding the cozy looking pink blanket that was draped over the rocking chair.

"What's limerence?" I asked.

"Basically, it's that state where you're infatuated with the new romantic interest in your life. Like, you can't stop thinking about them, or fantasizing about them. And you just really want them to feel the same way you do."

"That sounds like a crush." Clarke said.

"Do you have a crush on Northern?" Mecca questioned me.

I didn't even need to think about it. Of course I had a crush on Northern, but I wasn't here for talking about it at the moment. "Maybe." I said noncommittally.

Usually, I wouldn't hide my feelings from my cousins, and

I definitely wouldn't hide them from Clarke. I just wasn't up to talking about Northern and having them analyze every sentence and interaction that he and I had. There was enough of that on social media. My followers had somehow become his followers, and his followers had started following me. Now, every upload either of us made, every picture either of us posted, any comment we made online got us tagged, and invited speculation from every Tom, Dick and Harry about our relationship status. It was exhausting, and invasive.

I didn't know if it was greedy, or selfish, but all I wanted was a little piece of Northern that I could have to myself. Something that I didn't have to share with the world. That was probably why I couldn't stop thinking about Paris. About the time we spent in my apartment. About the sex. Those were the times that I had him alone. Had his undivided attention.

"Why are you even here this weekend?" Clarke asked me. Trust my twin to use her "twin-tuition" telepathy to read my mind. "Shouldn't you be in Atlanta somewhere, walking around Northern's mansion naked?"

"Right." Kyndall agreed. "Having shower sex. Or kitchen sex. Or hot tub sex."

"Or just regular bed sex." Joya added.

Clarke gave her the screw face. "Joy, I love you to pieces, but I promise that I don't see how you keep Nasir. You are so damn sexually repressed."

"Did y'all make all them babies in the missionary position?" Mecca teased.

I didn't care what Clarke and Mecca thought. I knew deep down inside that the whole innocent act that Joya put on was just that. An act. There was no way on earth that Nasir Payne wasn't waxing that ass anywhere he wanted, anyway he wanted. The streets liked to talk. If Nasir had cheated on Joya, she would've known about it. We would've known about it. The entire world would've known about it. The blogs and gossip sites would have been all too happy to exploit a scandal like that. Nasir was faithful to her. They had four children and were still rocking. She was not only giving Nasir the missionary.

"Maybe." She said coyly.

I rolled my eyes at her as hard as I could. "Whatever, liar. Y'all probably made them babies in your secret sex chamber, with a blindfold over your eyes, your feet shackled to the bedposts and your hands strapped to the headboard. Undercover freak ass."

I wasn't shocked at all when she smiled and gave me a salacious wink.

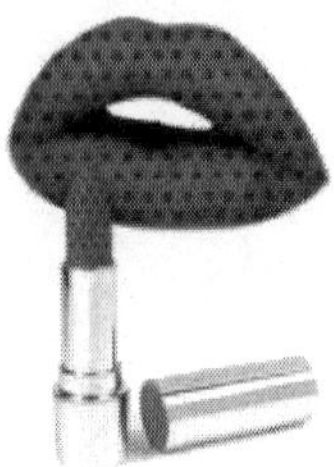

Although I enjoyed spending the day with my sister and my cousins, going home to an empty apartment was a downer. When Northern called me that night, I was still in a little bit of a mood. I gave one word responses to his questions, and just wasn't my normally talkative self. He let me get away with it for a minute, but eventually he got annoyed.

"Yo, what are you thinking, but not saying, Go?" He had started calling me "Go" as opposed to "GoGo."

I was silent for a second, then I climbed all the way into my feelings. "Why don't you want to see me? It's been a week. You haven't said anything about us getting together. Where are all of those plane tickets you were promising to buy for me?"

"Okay." He said slowly. "So, this is what we're doing. Got it."

"Don't do that, Northern. Don't act like I'm tripping." I said, even though I *knew* I was tripping.

"Are you even serious, right now?"

"Yeah, I'm serious."

"Can you get to the airport?" He asked.

"Wh...what?" I stammered. "It's 8:30 at night."

"Don't start backtracking, now. You're talking all that shit. Acting like my dick ain't been hard for you for seven straight days."

I smiled to myself.

I could hear him typing on a keyboard. "You're lucky the last flight left from O'hare at 6:20. But I'm putting your spoiled ass on the first flight out tomorrow morning. Pack a bag. I'll have you picked up at the airport as soon as your plane lands."

"You don't have to do that, Northern." I told him. I knew he probably thought I was bi-polar or something, but I was starting to feel kind of stupid for being such a brat.

He sighed heavily, like it took a lot of patience to deal with me calmly. “I wanna do it, Indigo. I should’ve done it days ago. I would’ve done it days ago, but I didn’t wanna scare you.” He sighed again. “There’s facets to my personality, Gorgeous. I tend to move fast. It’s a by-product of working in the music industry. When a beat feels good, I don’t spend time questioning it. I press. When the creativity is flowing, I roll with it. I’ll work 24 hours straight, for three weeks in a row if that’s how my creativity is flowing. I won’t stop. I won’t measure my output. I won’t look for balance. I’ll just go. That tends to pour over into my regular life. So, sometimes when things are flowing, when they feel good, I tend to push forward. You feel good to me, Indigo. I’m trying to hold myself back from going too fast for you. Sorry, if it came off like I didn’t want to see you. I just don’t want to scare you.”

“You’re not scaring me.” I assured him.

“Well, I told you that I would let you run the show. The only thing you told me, was that you just wanted sex. I have no idea how often you need it.”

“Everyday.” I mumbled softly to myself.

“I’m still learning you. If you wanna get knocked tell me,

I'll knock the shit outta you. Cuz I wanna fuck every single day. Multiple times a day. No cap. No exaggeration. Do you wanna get knocked?"

"You're so crass." I told him, shaking my head. "But yeah, I do."

"And you will." He promised me. "I'm headed out right now. Have a good night. I'll text you your flight itinerary."

"Bye. Northern." I hung up the phone, and went to grab a piece of luggage out of the closet.

Just like he promised, Northern had a driver meet me at the airport in Charleston, South Carolina. I was caught off guard when I got the text with my itinerary and it showed me flying into Charleston. I expected to fly into Atlanta. But it was whatever. I loved Charleston. And in early October, the weather was beautiful. Warm enough to enjoy the beach and ocean, but not hot enough to make me sticky or uncomfortable. I sat in the back of the black Cadillac Escalade watching the scenery rush past me through the tinted windows. Butterflies fluttered in my stomach in anticipation of seeing Northern.

He never told me what town his house was in, so it was a surprise when the driver turned off of the main drag, and took a road that led out to one of the barrier islands. I loved being on the coast. Like I shared with him, my parents owned a small beach bungalow on Isle of Palms. I spent my childhood vacationing on that particular island.

The sign welcoming me to Jackson Island was covered with sand, and surrounded by dune grass. A slow smile spread across my face, I felt like I was coming home.

Northern's house, if you could refer to the mini-palace on the beach as simply a "house," was set back from the road. The driver took me up a wide driveway, past a vast green lawn, glorious palm trees, and lush gardens of wildflowers. The house was impressive - set up on pilings to protect it from flooding in the event of a hurricane, painted a pale blue with white shutters that were secured with classic black shutter dogs. From the outside, the house didn't look like anything I would imagine Northern owning. It was formal, and grand. It did, however, fit in perfectly with the setting.

The truck came to a stop and the driver jumped out of his seat. It took everything in me not to jump out myself. Instead, I waited (impatiently) while the driver came around and opened my door for me. While he went to remove my luggage from the trunk, Northern appeared at the top of the stairs. Although he seemed far away, we made eye contact, and he left the porch, starting towards me. When he was close enough to touch me, he pulled me into his arms and hugged me tightly. I basically tried not to melt and/or drop my panties right there in the driveway. My stomach dipped and my heart lurched at the contact.

Nobody asked you to get involved. I told my rapidly beating heart. *Anyway, it's just the limerence.*

"I missed you." He whispered into my ear.

I appreciated that Northern never seemed to edit himself. He just said what he thought and what he felt.

"I missed you, too." I admitted. Then pulled his head down to mine, and slid my tongue into his sweet mouth.

We stood there, kissing in his crushed seashell covered driveway. I couldn't say how long the kiss actually lasted, but we did finally pull away from each other when the driver cleared his throat loudly. When my gaze drifted to him, he was standing there awkwardly, holding the handle of my luggage. Northern took it from his hand.

"Thank you." He told the dude.

"You're welcome. Have a good day." The driver responded, and headed back towards the truck.

I was confused. "He's not *your* driver?"

"I don't need a driver when I'm here. If I don't feel like driving, Rock drives me. I leave that stuff for Atlanta, where people recognize me, and know who I am and what I do. When I'm here, I can grocery shop, chill at the beach, whatever I wanna do, and nobody bothers me."

"So, you didn't bring security with you?"

He smirked. "I try to keep security at a minimum when I'm here. When I'm in Atlanta, yes - all day, security. When I'm in Chicago? Hell yeah, security. Plenty of it. In South Carolina, with all these blue blood billionaires and cats who've had money in their families since the 1700s? Not really."

"I think you should bring your security with you, Northern. It's better to be safe than sorry."

"I agree. That's why Rock is chilling in the apartment above the garage, but honestly I probably won't really use him." He kissed me on the lips. "Come on, Go. Let me show you the house."

After trudging behind him up one million stairs, I followed him inside the house. Where the exterior facade was traditional, oversized Carolina Coastal, the inside of the house was modern. Every wall was painted white, the trim was wood and the fixtures were black. The style was modern farmhouse causing the house to look like something that Joanna Gaines decorated. In juxtaposition to the house that looked like it had been decorated by a prim caucasian lady, Bryson Tiller's "Slept On You" was blasting through the house from invisible speakers. I smiled at that.

Northern led me into the dining room, which featured a wall of windows that looked out onto the ocean. A deck, dune grass and mere feet of sand separated the house from the shore. The view was breathtaking.

"Can I go on the deck?" I asked him. I knew he had to hear the excitement in my voice, because he gave me a dimpled grin.

"Can I show you where you're staying first?" He teased.

I calmed myself down. "Yes, you can."

I followed him up the stairs, where there was a long hallway. At the end of it were double doors that I would've bet money led to the master bedroom. On either side of the hallway, there were rooms. He explained to me what each one was as we approached it. Guest bedroom. Guest bedroom. Guest bedroom. Bathroom. Laundry room. Guest bedroom.

Silently, I wondered to myself why he needed so many guest bedrooms. Did he have children that he was keeping a secret?

"I like to host my family here during the holidays." He explained, as if reading my mind.

"Okay." I said softly.

When we got to the door that was closest to the mysterious double doored room, he stopped.

"You're staying in here."

"I'm not staying in your bedroom?" I asked, smirking. "What's good, Chocolate? You the type who gets uncomfortable when she spends the night? Don't like the thought of me crowding your space?"

"Maybe." He allowed. "Maybe I'm still learning you, and I wanted to give you your space. Maybe you're the type that gets uncomfortable when *he* spends the night."

"Whatever." I dismissed his attempt to feed me back to myself. "I noticed that you only got me a one way ticket. What? You trying to see how many days it takes for you to get tired of me? Then you'll send me home?"

He watched me with an odd look in his brown eyes. Kind of like he wanted to say something, but then thought better of it. "Indigo, you're welcome to stay in whatever room you want, for however long you want. Okay?"

"Okay." I said, with a firm nod.

"Fucking bully." He mumbled, and both of us laughed.

I stepped into the over-sized bedroom. It was modern and upscale. Like the rest of the house, three of the walls were painted white, the fourth wall was painted a slate blue. The trim matched the accent wall, slate blue. The queen sized bed was covered in a creamy vanilla colored down quilt, and throw pillows took over almost a third of it. Above the bed was a dreamy chandelier made of fabric and on the floor was a cream colored rug made of fur. I could see a doorway that led to the attached bathroom. As glamorous as the room was, I knew the bathroom would be just as lavish. At the moment, I didn't need the tour. I needed to be with Northern.

"This room is beautiful." I told him.

"And feminine. It reminds me of you." He took a beat. "That's why I put you in here."

I smiled at him. "So show me where we're gonna have our... playdates."

He took my hand and guided me to the double doors. He pushed them open, and revealed his sanctuary to me. The room was, wait for it...white. But the drapes were a charcoal gray, and the accent wall was made of gray wood. The bed was an oversized king, and I briefly wondered if he had to buy custom sheets to fit it. The rug under the huge bed was white with charcoal gray stripes, and I promise that after my eyes had taken in all of the decor, and the feel of the room, my mind thought, *home.*

It didn't look like any home I had ever lived in. My parents' home was sizable. It was a 4 bedroom Craftsman style home in the Beverly area on the South Side of Chicago. Their beach bungalow on Isle of Palms was cozy and quaint. My own condo was modern and semi-sleek, upscale and warm, but very different from the house I was standing in.

No. Northern's house definitely didn't look like home, it *felt* like home. That was a weird thought, so I didn't let it linger, or plant itself in my mind. I pushed it away as quickly as it came, and wandered into his walk-in closet. It was humongous. Larger than my office/studio, larger than most people's bedrooms. The wood in the closet and the fixtures were dark, but the room was light and bright. I looked up at the ceiling and saw three skylights up there.

"Ahhhh, you have skylights in here. I love the idea of natural light flooding a closet. Closets can be so dark. It's hard to see your clothes, and the color tones and stuff. That was a smart design choice." I sat down on the leather tufted bench and sighed. I looked up at Northern, who had followed me into the closet. "Yeah, I could live in here."

"You're gonna live in my closet?" He chuckled. "That's an interesting choice when you could just live in the *house* part of the house. You wanna see the laundry room? It's got three washers and three dryers. Maybe you wanna live in there. Warm. Or hell, the garage is really nice."

I waved him off. "Whatever."

"Just saying."

I sat there, enjoying just being with Northern after eight

days of being apart from him. That probably wasn't good. If I planned to keep things sexual, missing him like I did, and enjoying being with him like I did, probably weren't good ideas.

I needed to keep myself on track. I beckoned to him with my finger. "Come here."

He came closer. Stood over me, as I sat on the tufted bench. I reached out for the waistband of his jeans, and started to unfasten them. "I wanna...*play* in all this opulence."

He cocked an eyebrow. "In my closet?"

I was thinking that we would take our party to the bedroom, but whatever. "Your choice."

He took my hand, pulled me to him and kissed my lips. "Let's go."

He took me into the bedroom. I couldn't get naked fast enough, my clothing hit the floor in the blink of an eye.

Northern held my naked body to his, nipping me on the neck as he whispered, "I missed you."

My knees buckled. "I missed you, too."

"I don't wanna go any more entire weeks without seeing you." He nipped me, again. Then soothed the spot with licks and gentle kisses.

My panties, had I been wearing any, would've been completely drenched. As it was, I could feel the moisture starting to travel south. Soon, it would move down my legs. I felt Northern's fingers at the entrance of my vagina. My legs opened involuntarily and I moaned loudly when his finger slipped inside of me.

"You're so wet." He mumbled, adding another finger. "I love that you get so wet for me."

My head was somewhere off in the clouds, so I didn't respond. Couldn't respond. The next thing I knew, we were on the bed and I was flat on my back. I could guess what was coming next. So, I tried to prepare for it, but I could not get used to the feeling. First contact between Northern's tongue and my throbbing vagina always drove me wild. Deep licks that felt like euphoria caused my body to rack with pleasure while my back arched off of the mattress. His tongue traveled in and out of my entrance, working me into a virtual frenzy. I tried to savor the feelings of ecstasy that he was creating, because I knew that soon enough he was gonna focus his attention on my clit. Five minutes after that, I would come undone.

He was tonguing me so tenderly, that I was tied up in knots.

My hands were in my own hair, pulling on my braids so hard that I was a little scared that I was going to rip some out. It would've been a small price to pay, because at that moment, the only world that existed, existed in my vagina. Moans of pleasure sprang from my mouth and floated into the atmosphere. I gave my braids a break, taking my hands from my hair, and placing them on Northern's head. He didn't mind. He never minded when I pushed his face into me and held him hostage. All he cared about was that I got off. He wanted me to cum.

"Oooooohhhhh." I moaned, breathlessly, sounding good to my own ears.

I knew I sounded good to him, too, because he increased the force of his tongue action. I moaned again, but couldn't help it. I was on fire. He attached himself to my clit causing the rapidity and volume of my moans to increase. I could hear myself doing the absolute most and being super loud, but couldn't quiet myself if someone had offered me money to do so. Northern made me feel good as hell.

I moaned, screamed, thrashed around under him, and called his name until the fire inside me was extinguished by the eruption of liquid created by my orgasm. I laid there peacefully enjoying the feeling of him licking me clean.

He climbed up my body and kissed me hungrily. I wrapped my arms around him and kissed back. Somewhere in my mind

I heard a voice saying, *"I'm falling for this man."* That thought didn't get to marinate, because by then, he was rolling on a condom. He pushed inside of me, joining us together as one. I felt the familiar tingle of my orgasm starting to build, as Northern bit down on my shoulder. I dug my fingernails into his strong back, trying not to break the skin, but failing miserably.

How could this man make me cum two times in less than ten minutes? I didn't get it, but I was happy about it. I threw my hips up at him.

"Oh my God, Northern! This dick is sooooooooo good." I moaned.

"Fuck!" He responded, as he pounded into me. He leaned down and buried his face in my neck. I felt him nipping and kissing me there.

"Please Chocolate. No marks." I begged on a moan.

"There are gonna be marks, Ma." He said into my neck. "Your pussy's too good, Go. It's sooo good."

He pushed my legs open wider, my feet flat against the steel that was his chest, and he stroked me. After about the fourth stroke, I was caught up in the tsunami. The pleasure was almost unbearable. I teetered recklessly on the brink of reality and fantasy. My head spun, and I screamed while Northern signed his name in my vagina, and made it his own. After his release, he collapsed on top of me.

"What. The. Fuck." He said, his breathing still labored. He rolled off of me.

I didn't respond, I didn't have the ability. I couldn't even make intelligible words. I lay there just enjoying the crests and waves of bliss that I was experiencing. Coming with Northern was like nothing I had ever felt before.

"I'm never gonna be able to have sex with anybody else." I told him finally. "You're doing like, some other-worldly shit to me every time we get down. Why do orgasms with you feel like that?"

"I've gotta question for you. Is your pussy made of Northern McKinley kryptonite?"

I laughed out loud. "You're so crazy."

"Did we already agree that you can't give the ass to nobody else?"

"Yeah. We did."

"We might have to put that in writing. Cuz on my mama, it's gonna be a major problem if I find out that you're out here fucking other people."

"I'm not doing it to nobody else, Chocolate." I promised him, as my heart basked in his words.

He pulled me into his arms and held me. I relaxed into him, snuggling into his side resting my head on his shoulder, as he laid on his back. It felt so natural to lay in his arms. Like home.

Quit thinking that! I chastised myself.

I put my hand on his chest. He took my hand in his and kissed the center of my palm. I smiled sleepily. I was so satisfied and relaxed that I just wanted to close my eyes and let sleep overtake me.

"Don't fall asleep, Go." He said, as if reading my mind. The hand that rested on my right hip, shook me gently.

"Okay." I mumbled, and snuggled into him more deeply. I was halfway there.

"I need to feed you. You need to eat."

"I can stand to miss a few meals."

"Nah. Let's go get something to eat. I'll let you get some rest, later." He leaned over and kissed me on the cheek. "I promise."

I was hungry, so I agreed. Part of me wondered if I would agree to *anything* Northern McKinley suggested.

I climbed out of his big, old bed, and went to shower so that he could feed me.

CHAPTER SIX

Northern

I watched Indigo as she came down the stairs. She was freshly showered and had changed out of the leggings and t-shirt she was wearing when she arrived. She had on a t-shirt dress, white gym shoes and a blue jean jacket. Her long braids were in a ponytail, but they spilled around her shoulders.

As I watched her, a couple of thoughts went through my mind. The first was that she was gorgeous as hell. Her beauty was breathtaking. It wouldn't have been surprising to anybody who knew me that I was gone over this girl. The package she was wrapped up in was exactly what I like.

She was bright - and I wasn't talking about her intelligence. Her skin was bright. She was yellow. Light-skinned. A redbone. Whatever euphemism one wanted to use. Her eyes were a golden brown, expressive and warm. Her smile was big and all encompassing. Her lips were full and pink. Her frame was curvaceous, and had the ability to make me think illicit thoughts every time I looked at her. Her breasts had to be double Ds. Plus, she had a fat, round ass, and thick thighs. She wasn't pocket-sized, but she was short, about 5'4 or so. And she just had a lightness - a positivity about her. She seemed happy. I wanted that around me.

When I saw her in Paris, initially I was attracted to her looks. Hell, she was gorgeous, but then she had shown herself to me, and given herself to me. So far, I liked everything about her.

The second thought that went through my mind was that the idea that she only wanted sex from me was complete bullshit. Like I told her when she suggested it, I didn't want to brag, but I hadn't met the woman yet, who could make that happen. The heart always seemed to follow the pussy. Always.

Besides, I could tell just from spending that little bit of time with her and Clarke in Paris that she wasn't cut like that. She wasn't cut to smash and dash. Clarke...maybe. But Indigo had "relationship girl" written all over her. She was sensitive and even though I didn't know her background story, it was easy to see that she was inexperienced. I was pretty good at reading people, and Indigo gave off the vibe that whoever dude was that she was rebounding from with me, he was probably her high-school sweetheart or some shit.

"Hey." I said to her.

She trained her gorgeous smile on me. "Hey. It smells like fried chicken."

"Hot wings. They're in the oven."

"You cooked?" Her expression was quizzical.

"Nah, Babe." I assured her with a shake of my head. "I have a chef. Local lady. Comes over and cooks. Makes things, leaves them in the refrigerator or the freezer for me to heat at my convenience. She was here while we were upstairs getting it in."

Indigo's mouth fell open. "Oh no. Do you think she heard us?"

"Your loud ass?" I teased. "She definitely heard you."

She placed her pretty face in her hands. "I'm so embarrassed. I thought we were alone."

"You ain't gotta apologize." I paused, and shot her a wink. "I like how you sound when you're all into it. It's sexy as hell. That's not something you ever have to be embarrassed about." That was honesty, right there. Just thinking about how she sounded when she moaned could have me bricked up in ten seconds flat.

The timer on my oven went off before she could respond. I

grabbed an oven mitt, and lifted the tray of chicken wings from the oven, as well as the tray of oven fries.

"Those look so good. I'm starving." She told me. "Anything I can help you with?"

"You wanna grab us some bottled water out of the refrigerator? Oh, and grab the ranch, too."

She did as I asked, and placed the items on the kitchen island, next to the platters of chicken and French fries.

"Can we eat out on the deck?" She asked. "I've been dying to get closer to that water."

With the way her eyes shined every time she mentioned my deck and the water, there was no way on earth I was going to deny her. "Yep."

We took our plates and drinks out to the fire pit and sat down. It was almost 6:00 and the sun was low over the horizon. Time hadn't gone back, yet, so it would be light for a little longer.

She took in the view. "Man, it's gorgeous."

My eyes never left her face. "Yeah, it is."

We ate silently for a few minutes.

"So, we kind of missed some steps in the 'getting to know you' process."

I nodded. She was right. We fast tracked straight to sex, because that's what "playmates" did. But now, she wanted to get to know me. I smiled to myself. There was no way in hell this thing we had going on was going to stay purely sexual. "What do you wanna know, Go?"

"Everything."

"I'm Northern McKinley. I'm 34 years old. I'm a music producer. I've been doing it for about fourteen years professionally. I've got three sisters. Two are older, one is younger."

"When's your birthday?"

"December 31st. When's yours?"

"May 10th."

"Is Clarke your only sibling?"

"Nah, we've got a younger brother, Miles."

I grinned at her. "Mo Better Blues?"

"Yeah." She sighed. "My mom's kinda predictable, huh?"

I just chuckled.

"Anyway, I'm 27. I'm a social media influencer. I've been doing it for about six or seven years."

She told me a little about her upbringing. Her parents. Her goals. I told her about growing up as a Navy brat, until my parents finally chose to settle down in Chicago. She told me what it was like growing up as a twin. I told her what it was like growing up with three sisters.

"What'd you take from that experience?" She asked me. "Did it give you a special insight into women?"

"It did." I said thoughtfully. "When I was a shorty, my grandfather once told me that I would be a fool not to learn what I could about how women's minds work. He said that I had an opportunity that most men didn't, and that I should take advantage. So, I did. Besides, my older sisters think they're my mothers, so they've been in my business my whole life. Always questioning me about how I'm treating women. Offering unsolicited advice. Trying to mold me into someone they can be proud of."

"So, you're close with them?"

"Like I said, they both think that they're my mother. They're seven and five years older than me. So, I don't know how close I am to them, but I definitely respect them, and love them. I'm close to my younger sister, Skye, though. That's my partner in crime. My road dawg."

"Where'd you go to college, Chocolate?"

"Chocolate? You keep calling me that."

"I do." She agreed. "Because your skin reminds me of chocolate."

"I made the correlation." I said with a chuckle.

"Plus, I really, really like chocolate." She fucked me with her eyes a little bit. "It tastes delicious. It smells delicious. And it's a stress reliever."

"Oh yeah?"

She nodded.

"What makes you think that I went to college?"

"You do." She cocked her head to the side.

"South Carolina State."

"Ohhhh, okay. That makes so much sense."

"Yeah. I came here for college. Decided that I needed to live on the beach." I told her. "Where'd you go to college?"

"Started off at Notre Dame, that didn't work out. Ended up finishing at Hale Williams University in Virginia."

"What happened with Notre Dame? Too far from home?" I teased. Anybody from Chicago knew that it barely took two hours to get there by car.

"Nah." She munched thoughtfully on a French fry.

"Let's not do this, Indigo. Let's not do the shit where we keep information that might help us know each other better, to ourselves. Talk to me. What made you leave Notre Dame? That's a good school. Hard to get into. Most people wouldn't just leave the opportunity for that kind of education. Did it get too expensive?"

"I followed my boyfriend there. He went there to play football. Full-ride scholarship. Destined for the NFL. The whole stereotype. We got together in high school, when I was young and naive.

My Auntie Bo told me not to follow him to Notre Dame. She

said, 'GoGo, there's a big difference between hearing that your man is running around on you, and having to live that thing face to face.' I didn't listen, though. Mostly because I never thought he would 'run around' on me." She shook her head. "Young and dumb. I was young and dumb. He went down there early...for football and all. By the time I got there in August, the yard was already talking. Folks couldn't believe he had a girlfriend with all the screwing he was doing."

"Damn." I said sympathetically.

"Yeah, I thugged it out my first year. Once I got on campus, he slowed down on hoeing. Tried to keep his indiscretions on the low. But I was spending all of my time trying to police him. My grades were so bad, I was on academic probation. I was like, sad and lonely all of the time. It was just...bad. When summer was over, I didn't even try to go back to Notre Dame. My heart and my mental health couldn't take the strain. I just enrolled at Moraine Valley Community College. I needed to pull my grades up, anyway. There was no way another college was going to accept me sitting on a 1.9 GPA."

I nodded to encourage her to keep talking. The wind hadn't picked up, but she wrapped her arms around herself, like she was chilly.

"I got my grades up, and transferred to Hale Williams. Clarke was there, my cousins River, Reign, British, Quentin - hell practically my entire family was there. Hale Williams University is like, a family tradition. Most of my aunts, uncles and cousins chose to go there, but I bucked the system by following dude to Notre Dame, and I paid for it. After all of the drama of that first year, all I wanted to do was be with my twin and people who loved me." She sat back in her chair, like that was the end of the story.

"You and dude broke up after your first year of college?"

She took a long swig from her water bottle before she spoke again. "Kinda, sorta. We were *that* couple. You know? The one that keeps breaking up, then getting back together. Then breaking up, again, and getting back together. It was sickening, but I kept rocking with him. I 'loved' him." She gave me finger quotes at the word 'loved.' "There were times where we were together-together. I mean, he took me with him when he won the Chuck Bednarik Award for being voted the best defensive player of the year, his second year at Notre Dame. I was there when the Fighting Irish played in the Military Bowl. And I was right there, at the table with his mother, and his sister on draft day."

That was a twist that I hadn't seen coming. It didn't dawn on me that dude actually made it to the NFL. "Draft day? So, he made it? Okay."

"Yeah, he made it. Played for two years in Tampa Bay, hated it. Then he was traded to the Bears. His hometown team. He was happier than I had seen him in a while." She took another long swig from her water bottle. "He was hoier, too. Is that a word? Hoier? He was more of a ho than I had ever seen him be. We were on an indefinite break by that point."

"Friends with benefits?" I asked, taking a drink from my own water bottle.

"Friends. No damn benefits." She chuckled, but there was no humor in it. "We would talk from time to time. Text. FaceTime. We really were friends. He called me up one day out of the blue, and told me some old bullshit about me being the kind of chick 'you come back for.' I didn't have a clue as to what he was talking about. So, he explained that he was going to smash other women. He was going to get it in as much as he wanted to, and as much as he could. He couldn't help it, that's who he was and he wasn't about to deny himself his fun, because I wanted a fantasy relationship."

I tried not to choke on my water, as I imagined some nigga saying that to Skye.

"But when he was done playing," she continued, "he would come back for me. Marry me. Make a life with me. And I promise, all I could think about was this documentary that I saw on a famous NBA player who contracted the HIV. Jamaal wanted to go trick with his hoes, then come back to me with the HIV, like the NBA player did to his wife? I was like...no, thank you, Nigga.

I'm completely good."

"How'd he take that?"

"He brushed me off. Jamaal wasn't used to women denying him. I was probably the only chick who ever did." She paused and cut her eyes up to the sky. "I let him hang around, because he was familiar, and I knew what to expect from him. He probably kept me around, because I kept him grounded. I wouldn't let him get away with the trash that other women would let him get away with. Anyway, we never got to finish that particular conversation, even though for me, it was done. I wasn't signing up for the crap he was trying to offer me, but he still thought that he could win me. He told me that he had practice, he needed to get off the phone. Said that he would get back at me on Saturday. It was a bye-week. He didn't have a game that week, so presumably his weekend would be free. He died in a car accident on Friday night."

"Jamaal Kirksey? Are you talking about Jamaal Kirksey?" I questioned. I knew that story. Every person in Chicago knew the story of Jamaal Kirksey. The hometown boy that was murdering the game of football, and doing it for his hometown team. Chicagoans loved that dude. He could do no wrong. No wonder he didn't want to be tied down to Indigo, even as gorgeous and as sexy as she was. He probably had every chick in Cook County lining up to suck his dick.

She nodded. Her eyes were out on the horizon, now. The sun was much lower than it had been when we came out on the deck. Soon it would be completely gone, and the ocean would be pitch black. I would still have light on my deck, from the lanterns that my decorator insisted on putting out there, and from the fire pit - but the ocean itself would be dark.

"What happened?" I asked softly.

"Everything. I got the news from Clarke. They took him to Northwestern Hospital, and one of her friends worked in the ER there. So, I got there as quickly as I could. I found his family and I just stayed with them, waiting to get news - an update.

The doctors worked on him hard. No hospital wanted to be the hospital that lost Jamaal Kirksey. But he died. I mean, he was doing at least 60, and it was a head-on collision. The chick who was with him in the car, died on impact. That was a huge deal. The police swarmed the hospital, waiting to see if Jamaal would wake up so they could question him, get his statement. I was devastated when he died, but at the same time, I could see, even in the hospital how bad it would've been for him if he had lived. He was at the wheel and his passenger died. Plus, apparently she was giving him a 'head-banger' when the crash occurred."

I wasn't sure that I wanted to know, but I felt compelled to ask. "What makes you say that?"

"He had teeth lacerations on his penis. It was severed. Apparently, she bit down on it at impact."

"What???!!!??" I asked incredulously. "What??!!!"

"She was sucking him, and the impact of the crash caused her jaw to clamp down. I mean, the impact broke her neck, so she took the brunt of it."

"How can you say that?" I asked, grabbing my own dick and holding it gingerly. "How can you say that? If you practically get your dick bitten off, there's no way that someone else got the 'brunt' of the situation, Go."

"Uhm, Jamaal made it to the hospital alive. She didn't. I think she took the brunt of it, Chocolate."

"So, Jamaal Kirksey showed up at the hospital with his dick hanging off? Fuck." I couldn't even really wrap my mind around that. "I guess that part of the story never made the news."

"Hell no. As soon as his lawyer found out what happened, he made everybody who had anything to do with treating Jamaal sign a non-disclosure agreement. The entire situation was just gruesome, and tragic. Jamaal didn't deserve to die like that."

The devil on my shoulder whispered something about karma being a motherfucker, but I pushed that thought out of my mind. She was right. There weren't many people who deserved to die like Jamaal did, or especially like his passenger did.

I stood up from where I was seated, took her hand and pulled her up, as well. Then I guided us over to the edge of the deck. I leaned against the railing and wrapped my arms around her, so she wouldn't feel alone. Then, I looked into her pretty face.

"I'm the rebound guy for Jamaal Kirksey?"

"You're not the rebound guy, Northern."

"You told me that I was."

"I told you," she said, shaking her head, "that you weren't the rebound guy in the way that you were probably thinking. And you're not."

"You're over it? How do you get over something like that?"

"Time and effort. A lot of time, and a lot of effort. And I'm not over it, please believe me, but I am past it."

I figured there was more that she would say, if I gave her space. So, I released her from my embrace and turned my attention to the ocean. The waves were white-capped, but choppy and erratic. Beautiful, but dangerous. I wondered if there was irony in that.

She sighed heavily. "When the doctors told us that Jamaal was gone, we left the hospital like zombies. It was surreal. I went back to his mom's house with the rest of his family and we all just cried. The paparazzi and the press showed up like vultures wanting interviews, and statements. It was just a bad scene. A horrible scene. A scene I wouldn't wish on my worst enemy. Being there, in his mom's house with all that fresh misery and mourning, I never would've thought it could get any worse, but it did."

"What happened?"

"His publicist started talking."

"About what?"

"About public image. Jamaal was a black, rich, successful, professional athlete who had just killed a civilian. A white girl. A local girl-next-door. His publicist felt like that needed to be addressed."

"Did Jamaal know the chick? Did they have a *thing*?"

"He didn't know her. Her friends confirmed that he met her that night. Picked her up at *Beta Bar*. She damn sure didn't know him."

"Okay."

"Anybody and everybody who knew Jamaal, knew that he couldn't drive. I mean, he had a license, and he could drive...legally - but the practical application of driving, and doing it safely? Yeah, that was something his ass couldn't master. We teased him constantly about his lack of driving skills. He tore up every car he ever owned. I hated riding with him. He scared the hell outta me. If he was driving, I wouldn't talk to him. I wouldn't even let him listen to the radio. I would be like, 'Jamaal, you need to concentrate', and old girl was sucking him off, while he drove? She definitely didn't know him. If she had, she would've known that it would've been safer for her to suck him off while *she* drove."

"Hell nah. You didn't just say that. You did not just say that."

"I did." She assured me. "Anyway, this story is long and stuff, so let me cut to the chase. Jamaal's family decided to befriend the girl's family, and do some type of 'joint mourning' stuff. I knew his mom was in pain, so I assumed that she was clinging to the girl's mom, because they had both experienced losing a child. I was with that, but it was hard when they relegated me to organizing the sympathy cards, and the flowers and stuff.

I mean, Jamaal and I were on again/off again for years...and to be honest, we were mostly off. Still, we were friends. We were down for each other, even when we weren't together. His family knew that. His mother would tell me all of the time that I was her future daughter-in-law. She was just waiting for Jamaal to get his stuff together. Then, they pretty much pretended that I didn't exist, and that really bothered me." She paused. "That really hurt me, Northern. I didn't even know how to grieve for Jamaal, as it was. We had been through soooo many ups and downs. All the cheating. All the breaking up, and making up. All the insanity. Hell, we were in the middle of a fight when he died. But to have to watch them embrace a stranger and her family, while leaving me on the outside looking in..."

Pulling her into my arms again, I kissed the top of her head.

Her braids smelled like the cucumber and melon lotion that Skye used to wear in high school, a familiar, happy smell that caused me to inhale deeply. She clawed at me, her fingers sinking into the fabric of my shirt. Grabbing tightly, she pulled me as close as she possibly could and buried her face in my chest.

And me? I held her.

CHAPTER SEVEN

Indigo

I was shocked that I told Northern about what I'd been through with Jamaal's family after he died. The only other people who knew that story were Clarke, my parents, a few other trusted family members. Mostly I kept that hurt and humiliation to myself.

"I am not gonna cry about this." I announced.

"I don't want you to cry about it." Northern said in a tone that made me think he hadn't even considered that I might cry.

"Can we walk on the beach?"

I could feel the shift in his body as he adjusted to look down at me. "It's about to get really dark out there. Like pitch black."

"I know. I grew up coming to South Carolina. Remember? Besides, I have a flashlight on my phone. Come on. I just really need to be by the water right now. The ocean is my spirit animal."

I felt his chest rumble as he laughed quietly to himself. "The ocean is your spirit *animal*?"

"Yeah."

"Let me grab some real flashlights." As an afterthought, he added. "And get Rock's big ass to follow us. You don't hear me when I say that it's about to be pitch black out here."

Northern was right. The ocean was pitch black once the sun set. Way darker than I remembered it being as a child. I'm talking, I couldn't see anything that didn't fall directly under the beam of the flashlights that Northern, Rock the bodyguard, and I were carrying.

I could hear the roar of the waves and I could smell the saltiness of the water, though. That made me happy, that and the fact that Northern was holding my hand, and anchoring me. I didn't mind the darkness. I was just happy to be on the beach.

"Did you ever give yourself an opportunity to mourn for Jamaal?"

I smiled in the darkness. Northern let me cry all over his shoulder about the next man (I mean, I didn't literally cry, but I did unload everything that happened on him), and instead of being salty or jealous, he was concerned that I had gotten my opportunity to mourn.

"I did." I admitted. "I went to grief counseling. Three days a week, at first. I had a lot of guilt when Jamaal first died, because we were beefing and stuff all of the time. Counseling helped me deal with that."

We walked on the beach in the dark for about half an hour, but the weather had turned and it was chilly.

"I'm getting cold." I told Northern. "Can we head back to the house?"

Back at Northern's house, the two of us settled on the sofa in his family room. He covered us with a throw blanket, and turned on the television flipping through channels until we were watching "*Friday*." My bare feet were in his lap, and he was absent-mindedly massaging them.

"I talked so much today." I said.

"Don't even worry about it. I have three sisters, I'm used to women talking. Besides, I told you to tell me what I needed to know about you, and you did. Thank you."

"You're welcome." I took a few beats, opened my mouth, and shocked the hell out of myself with what I said. "You ever been tested for diseases and stuff?"

He stopped massaging my feet. "You ask the most unexpected questions. Yeah, I've been tested for diseases. I get tested every year for insurance purposes. Why're you asking me that, Indigo? You gonna let me stop using condoms or something?"

"Maybe."

"Have you ever been tested for disease and stuff?"

"Yeah, I have." I admitted. "My results are over a year old, but I haven't slept with anybody since then, besides you."

He resumed the foot massage.

"I'm on birth control, and I'm disease free." I continued. "I'm not saying that I want you to throw your condoms away tonight. We're just talking about it."

"Okay." He nodded his head. "I'm telling you right now, if you start letting me hit it raw, you're gonna fall in love."

"*Too late*," my subconscious told me. Out loud, I said, "whatever, narcissist."

"I'm not being narcissistic. I'm just telling you, raw dick'll change your life."

"Promises. Promises." I teased.

Northern and I hung out for about another hour, before I drifted off to sleep on the sofa in his family room, with my feet in his lap. I didn't know how long he let me sleep there, but I did remember him waking me up and leading me upstairs. I slept in the guest room. It was my intention to give Northern more sex, then fall asleep curled up beside him, but that hadn't happened. I had gone into the guest room to do my night-time routine, and I didn't make it out of there.

Now, it was just after 7:00am. I padded into the bathroom, used it, washed my hands, washed my face and brushed my teeth. Then, I made my way to the double doors.

They were wide open. I entered the room, and smiled when my eyes landed on Northern. He was still asleep, blanket balled up by his feet, completely naked.

What a beautiful man. I thought to myself as I crossed the room. I climbed in behind him and made myself comfortable. I reached down, below his waistline, feeling my way until my search was rewarded. Half-hard morning wood. I circled my fingers around his dick, and felt him start to grow. I crawled down his sexy body, pushing the crumpled blanket to the floor to make room for myself. I covered him with my mouth, bobbing my head as I took him into my throat.

"Huhmmmmm." I moaned.

I felt him shift slightly, before his hands buried themselves in my braids.

"Oh shit. You figured out my absolutely most favorite way to wake up in the morning."

I hummed against his dick, again.

"Fuck." He murmured. "You have no idea how good you look doing that, Go. You look like a fucking sex goddess."

I pulled back, then licked the vein on the underside of his thick shaft. I ran my tongue along the head, then tilted my head, taking him deep. When I couldn't fight the urge, I went ahead and swallowed. Northern's dick twitched in my throat, tickling me, and shooting a delicious twinge to my vagina. I needed and wanted more, so I slowly released him from my mouth, and climbed back up his body.

"Good morning." He told me with a dimpled smile.

"Good morning." I responded straddling him, my bare vagina against his pelvis.

"Why do you have on so many clothes?"

Actually, all I had on was a Hales Williams University t-shirt. I shot him a wink. "Anticipation."

"Next time. This time, lose the shirt."

I pulled it over my head and tossed it to the floor.

"Thank you." He told me. "I want to see you. I want to wake in the morning and see you, Indigo."

He wanted to wake up in the morning and see me? What the hell did that mean? Every morning? Just this morning?

My facial expression must've given away the fact that I was warring with myself. He clarified. "Every morning that you're with me, I wanna wake up and see you. *All* of you."

Got it. He wanted me naked in the morning. I could do that. "Okay." I agreed, easily. Then, I took him in my hand, lifted my body slightly, and positioned the head of his dick right at the bullseye.

I slid down, slowly impaling myself on him while my eyes rolled back in my head.

"You're fucking beautiful." His hands came to my waist. "And you feel like an inferno. I swear I don't get how you can be so hot, but so wet at the same time."

I placed my hands flat on his chest, and bounced. He felt like nirvana. Explosions were taking place that I couldn't control - behind my eyelids, in my mind, in my vagina. I was in my happy place. His hands moved from my waist to my nipples, squeezing them roughly while I bounced harder.

"You feel so good."

"Gimme a second." I responded on a moan. I sat straight up

and began to move my pelvis. Slowly at first. Delicately drawing first one letter S, then another. I repeated the movement a few times before I achieved the desired response from Northern.

"What the fuck?" He groaned, his hands flying to my waist.

I picked up my speed, watching as his face contorted in pleasure as I moved my pelvis and hips as sensually as I could. Northern pressed his hips up, his entire dick buried inside of me. We rode like that for what felt like an eternity until a slow moving storm started brewing inside of me.

I keened and whimpered softly trying to keep my composure, so that I could continue the rhythm. When he dug his fingers into my thighs, I threw my head back in ecstasy. I had never felt anything like the sensations that Northern was creating inside me.

I yelped loudly. "Yes! Yes!" I lost the rhythm, and proceeded to pound down on him, while he pounded up at me. Fireworks exploded behind my closed eyelids, while dynamite went off between my legs. Northern's hands were on my shoulders, pushing me further down on this throbbing dick, while streams of hot cum shot into me.

"Oh my God." I sighed, as I crashed down on his heaving chest. His dick was still jumping inside of me.

He hugged me to him. I kissed his lips.

"The things you do to me." I told him when we broke the

kiss.

"That's you." He pulled me down and kissed me again.

"I hate to move. It's gonna be a wet, leaky mess."

"But it was worth it."

Since my vagina was still tingling, I could admit that he was right. I slid off of him, liquid gushing out of me. That was the thing about deciding to ditch condoms.

"Sorry. Sorry." I apologized, as I collapsed beside him.

"You're cool. We'll change the sheets and it'll be like it never happened...until we make it happen again."

I rested my head on his shoulder.

"Ay, Gorgeous."

"Uh huh." I mumbled. Sleep was taking me under, I didn't hear another word he said.

I peeled my eyes open several hours later. Northern was wrapped around me, his dick pressed into my ass, one of his hands holding my left breast. I was aroused and my vagina felt achingly empty. I wiggled on his dick.

"You up?" He whispered.

"I'm up."

He lifted my left leg over his, and slipped easily inside me. I sighed with contentment. I could have sex with Northen a hundred times a day and never get tired of it. His hand left my breast and found my clit. A few minutes after that, we were caught up in mutual orgasms.

“We need to get out of this bed.” He told me, once we had both come back down to earth.

“I know. I’m starving.”

“Me too. Let’s go to Charleston. I’ll feed you.”

After we showered and dressed, Northern had Rock drive us to a restaurant called The Urbane Grille, over on King Street. I was starving, so everything on the menu looked good and I couldn’t decide what to eat. That must’ve been some kind of challenge to Northern, because he ordered some of everything in response to my indecisiveness. Shrimp & grits, jerked crab claws, fried chicken, biscuits & gravy, lobster cakes, crab rice.

“This is too much food.” I told him, giggling as the server

loaded dish after dish onto our table.

"Probably."

I took a little bit of everything, and each bite was delicious.

Northern looked across the table at me, his warm brown eyes meeting mine. "How long can I have you for, Indigo?"

It took everything in me not to respond with "Forever." I was purposefully and forcibly beating back the romantic feelings that were trying their hardest to develop for him. I wasn't sure if it was the mind-blowing sex that was crossing me up, the limerence, or Northern himself. But everything in me wanted that man. I wanted him to be mine. I wanted to be his. But it was too soon. I was moving too fast. I hadn't even known him that long.

"I'm thinking I should leave tomorrow." I said, taking a spoonful of crab rice into my mouth. The flavor exploded on my tastebuds.

"Why are you thinking that?" He asked, watching me.

It was hard to withstand the intense gaze of those eyes. "My upload schedule." I answered vaguely.

"Be for real. I know you have back-up videos that you can upload. You're a professional, Go. I know you have at least, what? A month's worth of back-up videos? Why are you really thinking about leaving tomorrow?"

I tried not to grin. He was right. I had plenty of back-up content for YouTube, and I could always post some pictures from Charleston and the view from his house on my IG. I shrugged my shoulders. "I don't know, Chocolate. I don't wanna overstay my welcome. I know you have things you could, probably should be doing. Instead, you're off playing with me."

"First of all, I like playing with you." He winked at me. "I wanna play with you all the time. All day. Every day. Second, you won't overstay your welcome. Not in two and a half days."

I cocked my head to the side, and lifted an eyebrow. "Do you have a specific number of days in mind that you want me to stay, Chocolate?"

"No, not specifically. I just want you for as long as I can have you. Two and a half days isn't long enough."

"Let's see how you feel tomorrow."

He pulled out his phone and started messing around with it. I kept eating, taking a nice sized bite of the jerked crab claw. About a minute later, my phone pinged with the tell-tale sign that I had a waiting text message. I knew it was from Northern. I cut my eyes at him as I pulled the phone from my purse.

"You're keeping me until Wednesday?" I asked with a smirk.

"Yeah. But if I miss you too much, I'm flying you back in on Thursday."

"I didn't bring enough clothes with me to stay until Wednesday." I lied.

"Good. You don't need to wear clothes. They just get in the damn way. I want you naked as much as possible."

Butterflies fluttered happily in my stomach. "Northern?"

"What's up?"

"How is it that you have all of this time to spend with me? I mean, shouldn't you be in the studio with your artists? What? Are you taking a week of vacation?"

"You know, for a lot of years, I lived my life around artists and the studio and a 'time is money' motto. I don't work like that any more. I pick and choose when, where and with who I work. Trust me, I do as little music producing as I can. I'm trying to back outta music."

"Why?" I asked.

He grinned at me, his dimples etching crevices in his chocolate cheeks. "Damn, your eyes got big."

"I'm surprised." I admitted. "You've been wildly successful in music."

"So, successful that neither you nor your twin even recognized me." He teased with a smirk.

"You didn't do it for the fame and recognition, though. You don't seem like that type."

"I did it, because I couldn't do anything else. It was a passion and an obsession, not a means to an end. Now, I'm not all that passionate, or obsessed over it. I've got my eye on another venture."

"Wanna talk about it?"

"It's not earth-shattering or anything. I've been restoring houses."

"It seems like everyone who gets into that just falls in love with it." I commented. "You doing it here? In South Carolina?"

He nodded slowly. "I've been doing it a lot on Jackson Island."

"Did you restore the house that you live in?"

"I did."

"It's beautiful. You did a good job."

"I had a lot of help, but thank you."

The server came by to check on us. Northern requested the check and carry-out containers. Once the bill had been settled, we stood up.

"Let's explore Charleston." I told him.

"What do you want to explore?"

I gave him a bright smile. "The market."

He looked up at the sky, then down at me. "How did I know you were gonna say that?"

In the backseat of Northern's Range Rover, while Rock drove,

I took my phone from my purse.

Northern brought his hand down, covering it, before I could start texting. He looked over at me with narrowed eyes. "Hey Indigo?"

"Yeah?"

"Tell me about what you were doing with your hips when you were riding me this morning. That didn't feel like you were spelling *coconut.*"

"Spelling coconut?" I repeated. "Since I don't even know what that means, I can assure you that I wasn't doing that."

"You've never heard that women will spell coconut when they're riding dick?"

"Uhm." I said thoughtfully. "Maybe that's why Jamaal stayed cheating. I wasn't hitting it right."

"Let me dispel that rumor right here, right now. Whatever the reason Jamaal had for cheating, it didn't have a damn thing to do with your sexual proficiency." He nipped at my ear lobe. "Getting you in bed was a fantasy."

"I was your fantasy, Chocolate?" I semi-joked.

"Hell yeah." He assured me. "The very first time I saw you, I was like, 'I want her'. And every time you get naked for me, I wonder how the fuck I got so lucky."

I shook my head. "Men and game."

He took my chin in his hands and turned my face towards

his. “You know that’s not game, Go.”

He kissed me deeply, and I melted, thankful that we were seated and not standing. My heart pounded in my chest.

“*Get a grip, Indigo*!” My brain told my heart. “*You’re not falling for dude.*”

“*You wanna bet?*” My heart responded.

“So, if you weren’t spelling coconut, what were you doing?” He asked, again.

“The figure 8.”

“The figure 8? You were making a number 8 on my dick?”

I laughed out loud. “Pretty much. It’s a move that I learned in this belly dancing class I took. It’s an isolation of the pelvis...”

“Hell yeah, it is.”

I laughed, again. “Uhm, seems like you enjoy that.”

He pulled me to him and buried his face in my neck. “I enjoy everything sexual that you do to me.”

My nipples sprang to life, and moisture started to pool between my legs. “If you keep doing that, we’re never gonna make it out of this truck.”

“Would that be so terrible?” He asked, nipping me.

“It would be fabulous, but I wanna go to the market.”

“What if I promise to bring you to the market tomorrow?” He nipped me again.

This time I found the strength somewhere deep inside of me,

and pushed him back. “Northern.” I whined.

He grinned at me. “Okay. Okay.” Then he looked me up and down hungrily. “But this ain’t over.”

The Charleston City Market was a historic outdoor venue. With hundreds of vendors represented, you could find all kinds of treasures and goodies. Mostly, I just liked to window shop and peruse the offerings. Northern held my hand, and hugged me to him as we shopped and browsed.

“Ay, did you bring a swimming suit?” He asked out of the blue.

“Why?” I asked, even though I had packed a swimsuit.

“I wanna go out on the water tomorrow.”

“Out on the water?”

“Yeah. On my boat.”

“Billionaires are just so casual with it, aren’t they?” I teased. “We’re going to be out on the water tomorrow.” I mimicked.

“I’m not a billionaire.” He said with a chuckle.

“How many hundreds are you short?”

He stopped walking, turned me to face him and kissed me on the lips. “Do you have a swimming suit with you or not? Cuz if not, I need to take you to get one, while we’re out here shopping.”

“We have a hard time staying on topic, don’t we?” I asked breathlessly.

"Because you fuck up my head. Make me lose my train of thought."

"Ditto." I agreed. "But yeah, I brought a swimming suit."

"So, can we wrap this up?" He gestured to the market area. "I'm ready to take you back to the house."

My panties instantly dampened. "Yeah, I'm good."

In the truck, on the ride back to his house, Northern pulled out his phone. So, I pulled out mine and shot Clarke a quick text since I hadn't spoken to her at all.

Me: ***I am fucking up so majorly.***

Clarke: ***Well look who's risen from the dead. Northern stopped smashing you long enough for you to text me?***

Me: ***Just for a minute. Then he needs me face down, ass up again.***

Clarke: ***Whatevs. How are you fucking up? You falling in love?***

Trust my twin to read my mind.

Me: ***So hard. So fast.***

Clarke: ***You scared?***

Me: ***Petrified. The sex is sooooo good, Twin. I mean, like soooo good. It's confusing me. I can't tell if I'm feeling him, or feeling the sex. I'm having all of these...emotions, and I can't tell if they're coming from my heart or coming from my coochie.***

Clark: ***You were feeling him in Paris, before you had sex with him. Y'all were moving fast as hell then, touching all over each*** *other, hugging all up with each other. You seemed cool with it, though. What changed?*

Me: ***Now I'm thinking it's scary freaky how fast we moved. Why was I all on his back in Paris, letting him feel me up under the table?***

Clarke: ***He was feeling on you under the table at dinner?!?!?!***

Me: ***Not feeling on me, feeling on me. His hand was on my thigh and stuff, not in my panties.***

Clarke: ***Not then, anyway.***

Me: ***Clarke!***

Clarke: ***If you want my opinion, I like you and Northern together. Y'all moved fast, but so what?***

I sent her an emoji of a shoulder shrug. I didn't know what to think.

Me: ***Wasn't like this w/Jamaal.***

Clarke: ***Again, so what? Every relationship is different. You would know that if you ever dated anybody besides Jamaal.***

Me: ***It's too fast to be falling for him.***

Clarke: ***I've got like 2 more minutes of patience for this convo, Twin. It takes as long as it takes. It seems like you're making this up as a reason to ghost him. If it was me, his fine ass would have to pry me off the dick. I can't relate to this "problem" you're having with the whole shit. He likes you, Twin.***

Me: ***He's rich and famous, Twin. He could get any chick.***

Clarke: ***Yep, and look who's there. Chilling in his mansion.***

Me: ****Le sigh* You're right. I'll text you later. ❤ya!***

Clarke: ***Don't complicate things by focusing on shit you can't control. Just enjoy yourself!***

I slid my phone back into my purse, and relaxed into the plush leather of the truck. Northern cut a sideways glance at me.

"You okay, Gorgeous?" He questioned.

"Yeah." I lied, with a fake smile.

He watched me resolutely, like he knew I wasn't being honest with him. "If something was on your mind, would you talk to me about it?"

"Yeah."

"Bullshit." He told me. "Do you wanna go home tomorrow?"

I didn't expect him to assume that I wanted to leave. I thought he would've guessed that I was falling for him.

"Nah. I'm good with staying until Wednesday." I took a beat. "I'm looking forward to staying until Wednesday."

Neither of us spoke. I stared blankly out the window, not really seeing anything. Northern went back to texting.

CHAPTER EIGHT

Northern

Skye: *She's pretty. And thick. She's exactly your type.*

Me: *In more ways than one.*

Skye: *Yuck. That sounds like sexual innuendo. You can keep that to yourself.*

Me: *You been stalking her Instagram?*

Skye: *And her YouTube and her Twitter. If she has you this open, I need to know who she is.*

Me: *What makes you think she has me open?*

Skye: *You, North. You keep talking to me about her, and that's rare. I'm thinking she must be amazing.*

I smiled to myself. That was why Skye was my road dawg. She was all light and love.

Me: ***She's dope.***

Skye: ***So why are you giving me your attention instead of giving it to her?***

Me: ***It's complicated.***

Skye: ***The way y'all were all hugged up in her Paris pictures, I can tell she likes you.***

Me: ***You sure about that?***

Skye: ***You're not? Why?***

Me: ***She's hot and cold.***

Skye: ***She's just scared.***

Me: ***Of what?***

Skye: ***I don't know. There's a lot of things to be scared of when you meet somebody you like. Fucking it up. Letting your past fuck it up. Unrequited feelings. Old baggage. Insecurities. Hell, and that's just off-top. Plus, you're like, rich and famous, Big Bro. That can be intimidating.***

I didn't respond right away. I was thinking. I wasn't normally one to rely heavily on superlatives or exaggerated platitudes and cliches.

She's different.

She has the best pussy ever.

I never felt like this before.

Saying shit like that just wasn't me, even if those thoughts were legitimate. I didn't like the idea of grading women against each other. Each woman I met was a unique individual and I did my best to try to treat them as such, the same way I would want a dude to treat my sisters like individuals.

I liked Indigo. I liked talking to her, and hanging out with her. We were a mood. She felt good to me. Good enough to make me want to free-fall into her, and that was something that I had never even considered, let alone tried to do. She was on some "stop and go" shit, though. It was frustrating as hell that she was holding back, because her holding herself back caused me to hold myself back, and all I wanted to do was flow .

Me: ***Is that why she's driving with two fucking feet, hitting the gas, then pumping the brake?***

Skye: ***Dayum. She got you over there pouting and in your feelings.***

Me: ***Later, Skye.***

She sent me a meme of some chick spitting water while laughing uproariously. I slid my phone into my pocket just as Rock pulled up to the house.

I turned to look at Indigo, finding her staring up at my house.

"What're you thinking about?"

"Just how pretty this whole setting is. Your house, the ocean. It's just really pretty."

"Nothing else?"

"Nah." She grinned.

She didn't want to tell me what was really on her mind, so I dropped it. "Come on." I took her hand. "I wanna ask you something."

When we got in the house, I led her past the kitchen and into my small home studio. Even though I swore that I was trying to back out of music, I'd had a studio put in when I was redoing the house.

She stood in the doorway, eyed the set-up, then eyed me. "Huh, I thought this was where you came to get away from music."

I laughed at myself. "Yeah. I thought that, too...but when we were finalizing the floor plans, I kept feeling like the house needed a studio. So, I put one in," I sighed heavily. "Honestly, I try not to use it, unless it's recreational. I try never to do business...to work while I'm here."

She walked into the room, and sat down on one of the stools.

I sat down next to her. "I've been on your YouTube channel a few times since Paris." I admitted.

She smiled at me. "I'm sure. Your followers seem to tag you

in everything I post."

"I think they think that I'm smashing you."

She laughed and nodded her head. "Probably."

"Anyway," I continued, "every time I'm on there, I can't help but notice your theme music."

"Yeah."

"Sounds like a 'Payne' track." I told her, referencing Nasir Payne, the music producer who was married to her cousin, Joya.

"It is." She admitted. "He did it for me way back when, like when I first started my channel. We keep saying that we're gonna get together and work on something new, but we haven't done it."

"Seven years later?" I teased.

"I know. We're trife. I'm trife."

"Would you let me put something together for you?"

Her warm brown eyes just about doubled in size. Indigo was so easy to read that it made me grin.

"Are you even serious right now?"

I nodded my head. "Yeah, I'm serious."

"Uh yeah, I would let you produce my intro track. That's not even something you had to ask me. You could've just sent me a link - like 'here's your new intro track, Go.' And I would've uploaded it immediately." She cocked her head to the side, her eyes were soft with emotion. "People pay hundreds of thousands for your tracks, Chocolate."

"They do."

"And you wanna *give* me a track for my intro?" She paused. "You are just giving it to me, right? Because you do know that I can not pay you for it."

"Consider it a gift. I have some ideas, but I need to sit with it for a minute. Come up with something suitable."

She slid her chair closer to mine. "You're cute. Acting like you've still gotta work to get the panties."

I laughed out loud. "I need to make sure that I'm worthy of the panties, Go."

Leaving her chair, she climbed onto my lap and straddled me. Her sundress billowed out, covering both of our thighs. Like she loved to do, she wiggled around on me until she could feel my dick pressing into her clit. Then she stilled for a few beats, before leaning forward and pulling my earlobe into her hot mouth.

"Damn, Go." I muttered, then pulled her face to mine and kissed her deeply.

Her arms came around my neck, as she returned my passion with heat of her own. I swore I could feel the damp sensation on my jeans, right where her pussy rested.

"Are you getting wet?" I slid my hand between our bodies and pushed her panties to the side, inserting my finger into her leaky vagina. Creaminess pooled around me.

She moaned.

"Fuck. Don't do that, Gorgeous. You know exactly how I'm gonna react to your pussy being wet."

"I wanna take my panties off." She said softly.

That shit was music to my ears. "Please take your panties off."

She stood up from my lap, quickly stepping out of her underwear. While she was doing that, I unfastened my jeans, letting them and my drawers hit the floor. She climbed back into my lap, slowly lowering herself down.

"Oooohhhh." She moaned, her face the picture of satisfaction. "You're perfect." She told me.

I grinded up slowly, while she grinded down slowly and the friction we created was paradise. Over and over I plunged into her, while she bounced down on me.

"Damn, this feels good." I said, placing my hands on her ass cheeks and lifting her a little. My dick sank deeper. "Right there."

"You always wanna be deeper."

"I always wanna be as deep as possible in you, Go." I palmed her ass cheeks, and lifted. I sank in a little deeper, even.

"Oh my God, I love this." She pressed herself into me, rolling her hips sexily.

She felt so fucking good. Attaching my lips to hers, I kissed her deeply.

"You're so wet." I said, breaking the kiss. "You don't know how bad I wanna put my mouth down there and taste you. But I can't pull out. You feel too good.

"I'm about to cum." She warned me.

"Me too."

Indigo's orgasm was hard and fierce. My orgasm was hard and blissful.

"Ahhhhhhhhh." I rode the waves of ecstasy.

"Yes. Yes. Yes." She chanted, as my dick jumped inside her warm confines and semen saturated her insides in spurts. "Oh my God, I love having sex with you." She pushed herself down on my deflating dick.

"Mutual. I could live with you sitting on my dick."

She laughed out loud.

"Or on my face."

"Imagine that."

I eyed her. "I do…all the time."

She leaned in and kissed my lips. "What am I supposed to do with you, Northern McKinley?"

I didn't respond to her question. I just pulled her body to mine and held her tightly.

The next day, we headed to the marina on the island to board my boat. She was being cool about it, but still seemed nervous. Especially when I told her that I would be driving the boat.

"It's not like it's a yacht, Go. It's just a medium size boat."

"And how did you learn to drive boats, Chocolate?"

We had parked my truck, and were on foot walking towards the dock where my boat was waiting. I stopped walking, and turned to face her, giving her my undivided attention.

"Listen, I know your last guy couldn't drive a car, and I know that scared the shit outta you. That's not what's happening here. I wouldn't take you out on a boat if I didn't know that I was capable of handling the boat. My father is a retired Naval Officer. He did 30 years in the military, and loves the water. He took us out on his boat as often as he could when I was a kid. He taught me everything he knows, and when I turned 18, I got my Illinois boating license."

"But it's the ocean, Northern."

I nodded in agreement. "It is, and I respect that. I'm safe. We're not gonna be doing no reckless shit, I promise you that. We're just gonna enjoy this beautiful day and chill. Okay?"

She sighed. "Okay."

Once we got away from the shore, she seemed to calm down and start to relax. The sun was high and the day was warm. I watched from the corner of my eye as she started to glide the cover-up she was wearing off of her shoulders. She hadn't let me see her bathing suit before we left the house, so I was waiting with anticipation to see how much or how little of her skin and curves were exposed.

"Is it okay if I go in the back of the boat?"

"Yeah." I agreed easily.

She had assured me that she was a strong swimmer, before we left the dock. That was the only reason that she didn't have on one of those bright orange, obnoxious ass life jackets. I immediately regretted that decision, when I saw her swimsuit. It was a one piece, but the middle was cut-out, exposing most of her stomach. I really regretted my decision when she laid across the bench seat in the back of the boat, her hand holding a digital camera.

I turned off the engine and met her in the back of the boat.

"What're you doing?" I asked innocently.

"Taking pictures."

"For what? For me?"

She chuckled. "To post on my social media, Chocolate."

"Hell no."

She twisted up her pretty face. "Hell no, what?"

"No thirst trapping ass pictures of you on social media."

"It's work. Don't be jealous." She kept snapping pictures.

It took everything in me not to grab that camera from her hand and toss it into the middle of the Atlantic. After a few seconds of silence from me, she finally looked up and studied my expression. She sighed heavily.

"Get outta your feelings, Northern McKinley. Yeah, once I post these pictures, niggas are gonna be in my DMs, but you're here with me right now. You're getting to see me live and in person in this swimsuit. My body is yours. You don't have to fantasize about me or drool over no image of me on your computer screen. You know this is my job. It's my job."

"Your job fucking sucks." I muttered.

"Sometimes, it does." She agreed, standing up from where she was sitting. I watched as she approached me, and wrapped her arms around my shoulders.

My hands automatically made their way to her ass.

"Would you take some pictures of me?"

I pushed her back, so that I could look into her face. "Dressed like that, in your swimsuit? For you to post on Instagram? Hell no!!"

"Come on. Chocolate. It's hard to get full-body shots when I'm doing selfies."

"Oh well, guess you won't be posting no full-body shots today."

"Ugh."

I took a deep breath. "Gimme a minute, Indigo. Let me think about it."

I walked away from her, and went back to the front of the boat. I sat down in the driver's seat, started the boat and let it cruise. A couple of things were going through my mind. First of all, I didn't want pictures of her in her swimsuit on the internet. That was me, being a man. I didn't want other niggas ogling her and drooling over what was mine. But she was right, it was her job. Part of her job was to look like she was living a lifestyle that other people should envy. That was her brand. Chilling on the back of a boat, while cruising on the ocean was enviable. How could I refuse to help her promote her brand?

I turned off the boat and rejoined her. "Give me the camera." I held out my hand.

She looked up at me and grinned. "You're going to take the pictures?"

"Yeah. Give me the camera, before I change my mind."

She went up on her tip-toes to place a kiss on my lips.

"No kissing on the boat." I said, my lips still against hers.

Her hand cupped my dick. "What about some of this?"

I caught her wrist softly. "Definitely none of that. Safety first." I sighed heavily. "Let's get this over with, before I change my mind."

We stayed out on the boat until a little past 4:00. The sun had been bright and strong all day long, seeming to zap the energy from Indigo. When we got back to the house, she went upstairs to take a nap, while I beelined to the deck to make some calls. As much as I liked to pretend that I was wrapping up my musical career, that wasn't completely accurate. I still had commitments and jobs on my books. I had been putting off work to "play" with Indigo. I didn't regret it. I would make the same decision a hundred times over, but that didn't negate the fact that I needed to give my business some attention.

I dialed up KJ Jamison. KJ was my A1 from day 1. We had grown up on the block together from little homies, to teenage troublemakers. KJ's MC skills, and my mastery of making those beats led us both to successful careers in the music industry. I was trying to do as little producing as I could, and still sustain a viable relevance in the industry. KJ had moved from focusing solely on his own career, to scouting and developing new talent.

"Ay." He said when he answered the phone.

"What's up? You still planning on bringing your artist through the studio on Friday?"

"Yeah. You gonna be there? I know how hard it is to get you in the studio nowadays."

"I'll be there for your artist. I'm leaving South Carolina on Thursday."

"We'll holler then."

"Later."

My alarm beeped, alerting me that someone had entered my house. I pulled up the camera on my phone, watching as Mrs.

Judy, my local chef, sat two bags of groceries on the counter.

Good. I thought to myself. *Because I already know Go's gonna be hungry when she wakes up.*

I chuckled to myself, at how many of my thoughts centered around Indigo and her needs being met. I shot Skye a quick text.

Me: ***I'm in my feelings.***

About a half an hour later, she replied with an emoji that was crying with laughter.

CHAPTER NINE

Northern

I made it back to Atlanta on Wednesday night and by Friday night, I was in my studio waiting for KJ and his artist to come through. It had been my intention to stay in South Carolina until Thursday, and normally, I wouldn't have been in any hurry to leave the state. The house I built there, the life I lived there were my escape, my peace. But damn, my house felt kinda hollow and empty without Indigo's energy.

Indigo. That was another damn reason that I didn't waste too much time before I hauled ass back to Atlanta. I needed to get my head in the game, and all my brain wanted to do was think about her, fantasize about her, reminisce about her.

I heard Rock, and my other bodyguard, Bull, talking to somebody, so I was pretty sure that KJ had arrived.

A few seconds later, he stepped into the "war room." He approached me with his hand out, slapping my outstretched hand and giving me a quick slap on the shoulder. "What's up, my dude?"

"What's up?" I responded.

Kristopher Jamison Jr was one of the first people I met when I moved to 73rd and Coles, on the South East Side of Chicago, as a shorty. We became friends in the way that most kids did. He was playing outside, I was playing outside, we started playing together. Next thing I knew, we were inseparable. He was tall, skinny, mischievous as hell and dark as hell just like me. The more often we hung out together, the more people asked us if we were brothers. Since I only had sisters, I figured a brother was something I needed, and KJ became my brother.

"So, who the hell is GoGoGoesGlam? That you?"

How to answer that question? I could be honest and tell him that Indigo and I were fuck-buddies, but something about that didn't feel good. I curved the question, but still managed to answer honestly.

"Trying to see where it goes."

"She's fine as hell."

I wasn't surprised to hear him say that. We had the exact same taste in women, had since we hit puberty. We both liked them bright, thick, and pretty in the face.

"You know why you think she's fine? She's Joya's younger cousin."

I watched while his eyes grew as big as saucers. "Shorty Songbird? Joya Bingham?"

"Joya Bingham-Payne." I chuckled.

"Fuck Payne." He said without malice. "Disrespectful ass. Getting my girl pregnant, then marrying her and shit."

"Was she your girl, though, Kris?" I couldn't help joking him. When he was on tour with Joya at the beginning of his career, all he talked about was how badly he wanted her. As his guy, I hoped that he would end up pulling her, but I knew it was a long-shot. Payne was a light-skinned, green eyed, pretty boy motherfucker, and she was already sprung on him. It was hard for Kris to compete with that.

"Fuck you, North. You know I loved me some Joya."

We chuckled together.

"You trying to see where things go with this chick, how're you feeling about her being posted up on Instagram in that swimming suit?"

KJ was my A1 since day 1, he knew me better than almost anybody.

"I took the pictures."

"You took the pictures?" He was appalled. His face was twisted into a mean grimace. "What made you do that shit?"

Chuckling at myself, I answered, "she needed full body shots, and she couldn't get them with selfies."

"She needed full body shots?"

"Stop repeating everything I say, Dude."

"Stop saying ridiculous shit." He countered.

"What's ridiculous about it? She's an influencer. She needed pictures for her social media. I took 'em. What's the problem?"

"You know how many niggas are probably in her DMs right now, because of some pictures you took and let her post on Instagram?"

"I ain't *let* her post them, Kris. It's her job. Her brand."

"Again, do you know how many niggas are probably in her DMs at this very moment, because of some pictures you took?"

I knew, and I didn't want to think about it. "Trust me, I know, and it's fucked up. But what was I gonna do? She asked me for help, was I gonna sit in my feelings and not help her? Motherfuckers gonna be in her DMs when she's fully dressed. I'm saying, she's bad as hell. Nothing I can do about that."

He shook his head at me, a smirk on his lips, "you're so fucking mature, Northern."

"Fuck you." I chuckled. "Ay, where's your artist? Time is money."

Hours later, once KJ and his artist left the studio, I spent some time online taking care of business. After that, I was basically dead on my feet, so I headed to the crib to lay it down.

The next morning I called Indigo. She had been on my mind all night, distracting me, detracting me, disturbing me. I had this gnawing thought that wouldn't leave me alone.

You need to make it concrete.

I wanted to pretend like I didn't understand what that meant, but I did. I knew that I needed to define this thing between us. I knew that just being her playmate was dissatisfying.

I'd spent practically my entire career in the industry "playing" with women. I was ready to chill. And even though I was fuzzy about exactly what that looked like, I definitely knew what it didn't look like. It didn't look like what I was doing with Indigo.

She answered on the third ring. "Hey Northern." She kinda sighed when she said it. I couldn't tell if she was tired, because it was early as hell, or if she didn't want to hear from me.

"Hey. Did I wake you up?"

"Nah. I'm up. I'm just sitting here...thinking about you." She didn't sound happy about that.

"You thinking about leaving me alone? Cutting me off from the good-good?" I held my breath as I waited for her to answer, realizing that if she said she was ending it, that would fuck me up.

"Nah."

"What're you thinking? You wanna talk about it, or should I leave it alone?"

She sighed again, like she had the weight of the world on her shoulders. "I'm thinking that I kinda played myself where you're concerned."

"Say less." I told her. I knew what she meant. I wasn't going to make her spell it out. "Being 'playmates' not giving you all the feels?" I teased.

"Shut up," she told me with a chuckle. She paused. "Wait, somebody's at my door."

I could hear her shuffling, like her slippers were dragging across the hardwood floor.

"Who would be at my door?" She muttered. Then, speaking in her typical tone, she asked, "is this you at my door, Northern McKinley?"

She flung it open, and came face to face with me. I ended the call.

"Good morning."

"Good morning. What are you doing here?"

"For real? That's what we're doing? I don't get a hug? A kiss? Just a 'what are you doing here'?"

She stepped into my arms tentatively. I wrapped her up ardently.

"I missed you." I told her. "Couldn't get you off my mind."

She tightened her embrace, but didn't speak.

"What's going on, Indigo? What has you up so early, and sounding all melancholy?"

Her face was buried in my chest when she spoke. It was one of those instances where you think the person speaking expects you to hear what they're saying, but maybe not really. Like they want to gloss over it, or something. I knew what she said, though. I wasn't sure if I heard it, if I felt the vibrations of the words from her lips against my sternum, or if I just sensed it. Whatever. I knew what she said.

"You're scared of me?" I repeated.

She pulled back a little bit, so her face wasn't plastered to my chest. "I don't mean it that way. I'm not scared of *you*. I'm scared of this." She gestured between the two of us. "Mostly I don't know how to do this. The only person I ever really "dated" was Jamaal, and we were 'off' as much as we were 'on', so I don't think that really counts."

"Ay, if you're expecting me to have all the answers, we're both fucked. I don't know how to do most of the shit I do, when I first start doing it. Luckily, I'mma quick study, and because I like to win, I'm usually dedicated to the process. Mostly though, I just do what I feel, and the majority of the time...that ends up working out for me. I don't have a lot of experience with like, dating relationships." I shrugged my shoulders, determined not to apologize for the way I lived my life before this moment. "All I know is that I like you. When I'm not with you, I wanna be with you."

"What if it's just the sex?"

"Do you think it's the sex?" I threw that ball right back into her corner. If there was one thing I knew about women, it was that sex added complications for them that it just didn't add for men.

"I don't know."

I looked down at her. The expression on her pretty face was just...sad.

"Listen, Go, I don't think it's just the sex. You feel good to me. We're a vibe. You felt good in Paris, in the taxi cab, at the restaurant, even before you let me hit. There was always that... chemistry. That magnetic pull. What're we doing about it? You gonna stand on this “I only wanna be playmates” lie or you gonna ask for what you really want?”

“I want to be more than playmates, Chocolate.”

“Good,” I said with a nod of my head. “Cuz being playmates is the last thing I’m interested in doing.”

“I want you to be mine.” She admitted.

“So, you gotta stop with the whole “hot/cold - stop/go” thing. If we’re doing this, then we’re doing it. You gotta be all in. You all in?”

Her brown eyes blazed with fire and eagerness. Immediately, I knew what she was on.

“You want some dick.” I accused. “I’m standing here trying to make a relationship with you that’s not based on sex, and you’re standing here thinking about banging out.”

“Your words are turning me on.” She whined.

“Let’s go.” I took her hand, and led her out of the foyer where we had been standing having our conversation.

“Where are we going?”

I gave her the screw face. “To the bedroom. I’m about to help you get this monkey off your back. Then, when we’re through, we can finish our conversation about how this relationship is not based on sex.”

THE END

AFTERWORD

If you enjoyed this book, please look out for my next release, "Keeping Busy", scheduled to release October 2020.

For updates & information visit me at:

Website = tracygraypresents.com
Facebook = facebook.com/authortracygray
Twitter = @alwaystracygray

Also, if you enjoyed this expression of my creativity, please leave a review at Amazon or Goodreads.

Thank you,

Light & Love

~ Tracy Gray

BOOKS BY THIS AUTHOR

Thugs Passion

To those on the outside looking in, Passion Hill seems to have it all. She's stunning, self-assured and spoiled. She looks and acts like she's living a charmed life. But looks can be deceiving. Passion's life has been anything but picture perfect. In her 23 years, she's lost a lot. At the age of nine, she was left to mourn her mother's brutal death at the hands of her father's enemies. Thirteen years later, she found herself standing over yet another gravesite crying bitter tears. This time, it was her boyfriend, Lorenzo who was stretched out in the casket. He too, was the victim of a vicious slaying. After facing the tragedy of losing Lorenzo, Passion makes a promise to herself. She's through messing with hustlers. No more misery and pain. She wants to close the door on that chapter of her life and move on. She's managed to put her life back together with the help of her father, her step mother and Lorenzo's best friend, Jinx Waters. For the first time in years, she's actually happy. She's determined to keep things moving in a positive direction by maintaining her stance on not messing with hustlers...until she meets Solomon Kent. Solomon Kent is everything Passion wants to avoid. He's unreliable. He's cocky. And he's a baller. He's the last thing she needs in her life. But he's also handsome, funny, sexy and GENEROUS. He's exactly what she needs in her life but at what cost? What's a woman to do when her head and her heart are at odds about what's best for her?

Heartbreak, Then Payne

Nasir Payne's ability to adapt has taken the twenty-six year old from criminal, to property investor, to up and coming music producer. When it comes to the ladies, Payne's green eyes, good looks, cocky swagger and self-assurance have made him successful without ever really having to actually commit. This works out perfectly for Payne, because after witnessing a crime of passion as a small child, committing to a female is the last thing he ever wants to do.

Joya Bingham is a definite go-getter. She's a hard-working, smart, self-confident, and beautiful flight-attendant. After enduring a relationship with an NBA player that was dominated with physical abuse and infidelity, Joya's faith in her own ability to recognize a good dude is left shaken. Jumping into another relationship will require risking her heart...and that is not something that the twenty-four year old beauty is willing to even consider.

When a chance encounter brings together a man who swears he will never love, and a female who swears that she will never love again, their attraction to one another is unmistakable. When murder, mayhem, deceit and lies are thrown into the mix, will this newly formed alliance be strong enough to weather the storm?

For The Love Of Gogo

Is it better to ask for what you want, or take what you know you can get?

Indigo Cross is sure about a lot of things. She's sure about all things beauty, She's sure that her 1 million+ social media followers respect her commentary, her reviews, and her authenticity. What she's not sure about is where to take things with Northern McKinley. So after a one night stand turns into... something else, she has no idea how to proceed.

Northern McKinley has never been confused about what he wants. He's always been the type of man to take what he wants from life and leave the rest. He took the music industry by storm. He's taken countless women by storm. Now, he's ready to try something different. How is it that he could finally be ready to explore relationships beyond sex, and the very woman that he wants to do that with, is only interested in the physical?

What will it take to get past the barrier that Indigo has around her heart?

Keeping Busy

They grew up together...but not really. More accurately, they grew up across the street from each other. He spent his youth pretending like she didn't exist. She spent hers pretending to be unbothered by his lack of interest.

Maddox "Busy" Mayhew dedicated himself to setting goals and reaching them. So, being drafted to the league wasn't a surprise to anybody. The fact that he was a savage on the football field, and crushed records wasn't a surprise to anybody. The fact that he garnered the attention of countless women wasn't a surprise to anybody. His fall from grace, though...that caught everybody off guard, including him. Now, he had to repair the damage he'd done, but frustratingly, he couldn't do it alone.

Mecca Goode minded her own business, and there was plenty of that to mind. Not only was she part owner of a hugely successful dance academy, she also choreographed for both collegiate and professional athletic teams on the side. She didn't have time to keep up with the happenings of old childhood neighbors, except when their demise was playing out in the public arena.

When a revered family member asks Mecca to step up to help Busy out, her immediate response is a thundering "No thank you." He spent years never even acknowledging her existence.

Will she turn the other cheek, and help out a man who spent his entire life ignoring her?

How will Busy handle realizing that the woman he spent a lifetime avoiding might be the very thing he's needed all of this time?

Made in the USA
Columbia, SC
02 July 2022

62651628R00102